# The Blessings of Hard-Used Angels

# The Blessings of Hard-Used Angels

John Cottle

*Texas Review* Press
Huntsville, Texas

FIRST EDITION, 2004



ACKNOWLEDGMENTS:

"A Christian Burial" first appeared in *Amaryllis*, 2000, under the name "One Long and Distant Shadow"; "The Girl at the Fountain" first appeared in *Literary Potpourri*, January 2002; "Nocturnal Birds" first appeared in the anthology *Working Hard for the Money: America's Working Poor in Stories, Poems, and Photos* (Bottom Dog Press, 2002); "Make me an Angel" first appeared in *The Clark College 2003 Writers Poetry and Fiction Contest Chapbook*; "Aftermath" first appeared in *The Alalitcom*, 2003; "Sailing into Orion" first appeared in *Ink Pot*, Spring 2004, special edition; "Sabbath" was published in *The Texas Review*.

**Cover photo of old Tallassee, AL mill by Amber Dickenson**

**Photograph of John Cottle by Suzannah Solomon Wilson**

**Cover design by Paul Ruffin**

**Visit John Cottle's website at www.johncottle.net**

**Library of Congress Cataloging-in-Publication Data**

Cottle, John, 1952-
The blessings of hard-used angels / John Cottle.-- 1st ed.
p. cm.
ISBN 1-881515-67-2 (alk. paper)
1. Southern States--Social life and customs--Fiction. I. Title.
PS3603.O869B58 2004
813'.6--dc22

2004002847

To Nancy

**With Gratitude:**

First thanks go to Nancy Cottle, my own dear angel and number-one editor, an impatient woman by nature who always found graceful ways to endure the sundry madnesses of mine that erupted as these stories were being born.

Thanks to Paul Ruffin and the people at Texas Review Press for all they did to bring this book to life. And my heartfelt thanks to George Garrett for selecting this manuscript for the prize that bears his name.

Thanks to Jeanie Thompson and the Alabama Writers' Forum for the assistance they gave me and for their support of Alabama writers.

The wonderful cover photograph was taken by Amber Dickinson, to whom I am deeply grateful. I predict a hugely successful career in photography for her. And thanks to Suzy Solomon Wilson, an accomplished photographer, for the back-cover photograph of me.

I cannot close without also thanking Francis Ford Coppola and the people at the Zoetrope Virtual Studio for providing the place where I learned the art and craft of writing fiction. There are so many there who taught me so much and who had a hand in the editing and the many rewrites of these stories that I cannot possibly name them all. But to Bev Jackson, Jai Clare, Luis Nunez, Tom Saunders, Donna Storey, Donna Ferrara, Brian Burch, Avital Gad-Cykman, Alexandra Thompson, Mary McCluskey, Sue O'Neill, and especially to Maryanne Stah1, I am forever grateful for your insightful critiques and guidance. May the Hard-Used Angels bless you all.

# Table of Contents

# Chele Kula

In 1809, the Turkish pasha Hurshid, commander of the town of Nis, duly memorialized his victory over Serbian Duke Stevan Sindjelic and his band of 3000 rebels by ordering the erection of Chele Kula, a structure referred to as a tower, though it is no more than at most three stories tall. From the outside, it appears innocuous enough—attractive, but not provocatively so, squared at its base with entries on all sides, rising into an octagonal arrangement with a roof that hips upward at a slight pitch, triangling toward a central pinnacle. It was in the spring of the year when Melanie and I were there, sometime in the 1980s, as I remember. The tower was surrounded with plantings of red and white flowers of a variety unknown to us, and the image of the structure, set among the explosion of vibrant flora, was a quiet salve to the eye. Upon our entry, however, we were struck by an urgent alteration in the structure's humor. There was a dank, mordant chill to the air, and an odor that suggested the presence of artifacts of antiquity. The interior walls were of a blanched and limey white—a jarring, colorless vacuum that sucked upon our eyes like a sudden blinding storm. I was overcome with a distinct sensation that something wicked was at hand, that it had long been loitering about, dating back to some vague and unreckonable past, and I was singularly cognizant of how starkly this setting reaffirmed Melville's thesis that the nonattendance of color in a thing is the true harbinger of evil. Melanie brushed against me and took my hand.

Though we had been told what we would find here, it nevertheless took a moment for the enormity of it to settle. Nine hundred fifty-two human skulls—someone had mentioned the number, though neither of us pretended to count—each set in its own row and column, some nearly flush with the surfacemortar so that they appeared to be looking through from the other side of the wall, others convexing outward, leaving a hollow bowl into which a wren's nest might suitably fit, the socket-hollows gaping blankly, the expressions implacable, those marrowless bones that once housed the conscious musings of 952 souls now reduced to building material. I recall there being little wind that day, but there was a strange, shadowy moan that came lazing through upon what slight breeze there was—a long, faint wail with a resonance akin to that of distant voices. It could have been no more than the whistling of baffled air, but seemed, quite reasonably at the time, to be of a more mythical origin. Melanie and I turned to each other as we heard it. Speechless within our own joint and curious amazement, we listened.

You take something away from such a moment as that, something that rides with you along the soft back of time and affects, in some small and inscrutable measure, the way you gauge the world, the way you size right and wrong, goodness and evil. I am not certain why this should be. The tower is, after all, a thing that may be learned of from books and without the disturbance that attends an actual viewing. I can only tell you that it is different to drink the disquieting milk of Pasha Hurshid's tower with your own brooding eye, that memory's echoes of the place weigh upon that fragile balance at the mind's center where morality is assessed, that they shift and recalibrate the standard in some slight way. Apprehension amends reality—nothing save death is irrevocable, nothing immutable.

I was a respected lawyer once. Until the Royce Macky case. The day I was obliged to argue his innocence to a jury was one worthy of a noon walk—one of those rare late-June Fridays when the air was light and brushed with an arid quickness so foreign to an Alabama summer. I remember the children on the square, skipping ropes and chanting rhymes, old men smoking on the benches, pert-breasted mothers pushing strollers, a satellite truck from WTSM parked before the courthouse, two wheels set awkwardly upon the sidewalk, and there was a freshness in the yellow sunlight and in the deep shadows of the water oaks that belied the weight of that duty I carried.

I'd eaten lunch at Cullie's on the Square, a pork chop, some greens and peas, watched young Kevin Marris fork the last oily flakes of his catfish from the bones, shared a pitcher of tea with him as we pretended to discuss strategy. Having been attached to more than my fair stake of hopeless causes, I could read the future. Age and experience have a way of winnowing down the randomness of chance. Not so with Kevin, who was bound to his recent legal education by a short chain of time that had yet to accumulate the first rust stains. He was still mired in a noisy present that continuously overflowed with desultory possibilities. I let him talk, let him nurse along his improbable theories of how the jury might process all of the fury and tumult they'd been served up over the past four and a half days, let him prattle on about the credibility of this or that witness, or the juror on the back row who had, throughout the trial, caustically leered at Bridgeport, the prosecutor. He's a good kid, Kevin. I confess to a certain relief when Carlton appointed him my co-counsel. It made for a quaint symbiosis. I was too damned old to be toting around a man's life on my lone back, even if it *were* only the life of Royce Macky, and Kevin brought a dynamic of gullible optimism to the case that was not all bad and that I could never have riven up from my own gut.

"They don't like Yarborough," he said. "I watched 'em close when he was on the stand. You need to hit on him hard." An agate-eyed squirrel scrapped across the sidewalk ahead of us, turned to look back disdainfully, maybe with a degree of fright too. I understood him.

"What can I tell you about Cy Yarborough, ladies and gentlemen?" I began. "An admitted killer who purchased his own life with his testimony in this case. How many people ever get such a chance—to purchase their own lives? Not me. Not Judge Carlton Speaker there. None of you, I'll wager. But Cy Yarborough did. And what did he pay for it? Just took the stand and told you how he and two people he didn't even know, and couldn't even remember, murdered Jamal Manderson. They killed Manderson and they tried to kill Reed Brown, and then Yarborough comes in here and throws out Royce Macky's name. Makes up a story and gives you the bend of his index finger that he aimed like a crooked snake at Royce Macky, and closed his deal with the prosecutor. And suddenly . . . *suddenly* . . . ."

"The death penalty goes away," Marris picked up. "Suddenly, the death penalty goes away and now Yarborough gets life. A life sentence he bought by testifying against Royce Macky. How can you *possibly* believe the word of a man like that?"

"Now tell me," I said to him, "how would you go after Reed Brown?"

"It was night," he said. "It was dark. No moon. He was scared, terrified. Frenzied even. How could he be sure it was Macky? How could he be sure?"

"And what about these other two bloodthirsties, ladies and gentlemen? The two nameless ones that Yarborough says were there. Where are they now? Why didn't the state find them? What would they say if they were here? How would they testify?"

They would say, of course, that Royce Macky was their leader and that he had put the noose around Jamal Manderson's neck with his own two hands and that he had jerked the rope with those selfsame hands until Jamal Manderson's feet rose free of the sound and trustworthy earth to thrash about like malfunctioning windmill blades. They would say it not so much because it was true but because it is in the nature of the human condition to seek survival and avoid annihilation, and so, like Cy Yarborough, they would make their deals and confess themselves with the messianic conviction of saved sinners, cottoning up to the notion that they were redeeming their lives rather than negotiating them.

We entered the courthouse under the west portico, the breeze following us into the foyer like a brace of ghostly hounds. The clerks and office workers eyed us as we crossed, we, the men-of-the-moment, Sebastian Tarver, dean of the Tykesville, Alabama legal fraternity, and Kevin Marris, his servile acolyte. They spoke to us politely, probed our faces for the mercenary obsessions they expected to find there. Cindy Abrams, the WTSM reporter, approached with a microphone. I brushed her off, told her later.

As we neared the stairs, we were forced to pass by a few members of the Manderson family: Jamal's mother, an aunt, a few others I didn't know. I caught onto the mother's eyes and nodded solemnly. She acknowledged with a slight head-bob, no words exchanged, no smiles shared. I knew the look, that unstable marriage of respect and contempt competing beneath those dark, assiduous pools. And she knew that I knew, and I knew that she knew I knew, and so on and on, like in an old-fashioned barbershop with mirrors on either wall where you can look down through an infinity of reflections and never get to the end of it, because either your vision is not acute enough to see so far or because maybe there is no end of it to get to—I'm not sure which it is anymore.

"Fifteen minutes," said young Marris. "Anything you want me to do?" We took our seats at the counsel table. The courtroom was empty.

"You know," I said. "There was a time when we would have won this case."

He looked at me blankly.

"Time was when anybody, even a young fellow like you, even an old drunk fart like Brody Ezell, anybody who could have picked up a file and stood half erect before the twelve white men who would have sat in those chairs there, anybody who could lean one word up against another just halfway artfully enough to remind them—*obliquely* remind them—about whose skin was what color, anybody who could have done that would have won this case. If winning is what you want to call it."

He looked at me with a kind of diffident uncertainty. "You're right, of course. But you can't go back there now. You've got this jury . . . a 1990s jury . . . ."

"I can go any goddamn where I want to," I said. He needed shocking, I thought. "I can go back there because I lived through it. Was a part of it. A cog in the machinery of it."

The lines and arcs of his youth began to bend into

seasoned layers of questions. "I know what you're saying," he said. "Back then it was wrong. It was broken. But it got fixed. Or at least, somewhat, it got fixed. Nothing's perfect though, is it? But it's different now. Those old appeals, they don't work anymore. And that's as it should be. But you . . . you've got to . . . now, you've got to . . . ."

"Do what?" I asked. "The same thing? The same thing but with different words than would have worked forty years ago? Different words, but aiming to the same result?"

A steel tunnel of silence connected our eyes. He was thinking how could he tell me something about Royce Macky, thinking how could he tell me that this icy-eyed architect of a mob murder deserved the best I could give him because of no reason other than it's the way of the system, thinking that he deserved it even if he hadn't paid for it, even if the State of Alabama were paying for it because Royce Macky couldn't afford to, and underneath all of that, he was thinking about how Royce Macky didn't really deserve to lick up the heavings of an ill-bred sow and trying to maintain that hermetic separation between what he wanted to tell me and what was bubbling just underneath what he wanted to tell me.

When he found what he was looking for, he turned away. He knew that I had it, saw that I was ready to spend it, saw that I would never be free to do anything *but* spend it, even if it were going to be applied to the account of Royce Macky, I had to spend it. And he was right.

It's like you've got only so much of it and you've got to let it out slow because when it's gone it's gone and if you waste it it's gone, and a young man might can come by more of it—might can, but it's not for certain—but an old man's only got what he's got of it and nowhere to go for restocking. I wouldn't call it integrity, exactly. Or credibility, or even respectability. I wouldn't give it a name at all, not out of the words there are to pick from. Something of it inherited, something of it acquired, and if you could give it a name then you could possess it and know it and tell somebody else you had it, and *that* somebody else would know that you had it and what it was you possessed.

My great-grandfather was the first doctor in Tykesville.

He picked lead from the flesh of Confederate soldiers with steel forceps and sawed away their mangled limbs with no more for anesthesia than a bite-rag and a few drams of whisky. My grandfather had a tintype of him in his office that he gave to my father for his office that he gave to me for my office but that I, to punctuate my total severance with three generations of Hippocratic tradition, kept at home atop Melanie's piano. My mother was a well-published poet, her brother, a New York stage-actor. I took what I was given of it, that of it carried by blood, added something of my own to it, back when I was young enough to supplement it, because when you're old, you've got what you've got of it and nothing to do but let it out slowly. Not exactly respectability or credibility, or even dignity or courage, but something of it you're given and something of it you take, and something of it in the blood and something of it without the blood, and Royce Macky watching me tip it out, watching me stand before eight men and four women and nine whitepeople and three blackpeople and tip it out, and him not giving a good goddamn about it or where it came from or how I was losing what I possessed of it, bleeding it away for him, and him looking at me with an irascible eye and a magnificent, sardonic smile, and the men and women and whitepeople and blackpeople studying and weighing and measuring and figuring.

It took them three hours.

Saviors are always betrayed in the final act—that's what he said to me the first time we met, sitting in his jailhouse jumpsuit, impervious and stoic amid the clanging steel.

"So this is about a death wish," I said to him. "You . . . a martyr for the white race."

"I never sought martyrdom," he said. "But if it comes to me . . . ." He looked away and shrugged.

"It seems to be on the way."

"But why should it? Why should it, when the State of Alabama has given me the great Bass Tarver to argue my case?" He laughed disdainfully. "Save my ass, counselor. Save my ass from that yellow chair."

"I'll need your help."

"Be glad to do what I can . . . ." He spread his arms, palms upward. "From here in my office."

"You can start by giving me the names of your two buddies that got away."

He let go a loud, hooting laugh. "Now that's a good one, Mr. Bass. Give you the names of the two that got away. That's good."

"Your case can't be won," I said. "Their evidence is overwhelming. Yarborough's made a deal. He's gonna sing. Reed Brown's gonna identify you. Your only hope is to bargain for life without. And if you wanna do that, you've gotta give 'em something they want."

"Life without, huh?"

"It's the best you can hope for."

"Well, fuck that. Fuck that."

"You warming to the idea of electrocution?"

"I don't fear death," he said. "I'm prepared to forfeit my life."

"And for what?" I asked him.

"I have this vision of the future. I see a world where the strong are free to be strong. Where the weak and inferior are pushed aside and the superior have their reign."

"That's been tried before. It's a stale philosophy."

"But we've only seen the seeds of it until now. Just the seeds. They've never been germinated. Never been nurtured and watered."

"So then along comes Royce Macky to water them. And with blood, too. But with somebody else's blood, of course."

He cocked his head at me in a cool, *sang-froid* pose. "Sometimes it takes blood, sometimes patience. You have to know what's right for the moment."

"It seems you miscalculated."

"Shhh! With those niggers, you mean? I don't think so. Only that we let that one called Reed get away. That was Yarborough's fault."

"So tell me," I said. "If the state pulls the switch on you, how does that advance your cause?"

"Many will fall before the final victory. I never expected to see it in my lifetime."

I looked at him across the steel table, relaxed backward in my chair. "It's a scary vision you've got, Macky," I said. "People being grabbed up at midnight . . . lynched for no reason apart from their skin color. Hardly a utopia."

"But we're only just now beginning the struggle, you see. The lynchings, the terror, they won't always be necessary. But first, the order has to be established. The strong . . . the physically and mentally superior—"

"The white race, you're referring to?"

"The Caucasian race, yes. It must be recognized as superior. It must ascend to its rightful place in the new order."

"At the top, of course."

"Of course. And then we can begin to restructure. To build a society where the strong . . . the gifted . . . can take control. Can you imagine it for a moment, the weak and inferior cast aside, all the world's resources at the disposal of the supreme Aryan race, all put to scientific and technological research instead of being thrown away on all the worthless niggers and wetbacks and half-breed mongrel races? Can you imagine the progress? Can you imagine such a world?"

"No," I said. "No, I can't even begin to imagine such a thing as that."

"Then you have no foresight. You have no vision."

"I think you're evil," I told him. "Purely and completely evil."

"And why is that?" he asked. "Why is my vision so evil and yours, if you've even got one, so damn righteous? What is it that makes you call a thing evil, anyway?"

"I came here to save your life. Not to discuss your odious philosophy."

"*Leave* if you don't want to discuss it. Just walk away."

"You're going to be convicted of capital murder," I told him, rising to call the guard. "There's not much I can do about that. But if you help me, I can argue for your life. You think about that, Macky. Life without parole or electrocution. You think that over carefully."

His eyes were lit with vibrant intelligence, his comportment well-reined. He had the look of a man in charge of his fate—the sheer antithesis of vulnerability. "You make your arguments, counselor," he said. "You look that jury in the eye and make your arguments. You make 'em strong and you make 'em persuasive. You can do it. You've done it before. You tell that jury there's not enough evidence to convict me. You convince 'em the face that nigger saw out there that night wasn't mine. You get my ass outta this. That's your job. I ain't talking with you about life without parole or giving up anybody. You just win my case and get my ass outta this jail."

What arguments can you make for such a boy—such a man, I should call him? I had the weekend to consider. We were due back in court on Monday morning for the sentencing phase, the jury having accomplished the perfunctory task of finding him guilty as charged. His freedom now permanently forfeited, it only remained to be decided whether he would be let to live in captivity or culled from the population. We would be ready, young Marris and I, set to present our well-rehearsed snapshot of our client's rearing: the insane uncle who took him in after his father killed his mother and disappeared from the face of the earth, the bilious preachings of the surrogate father and how they shaped and wasted his above-average intellect, the jagged, disassociated childhood of this self-educated boy who needed no more than a challenge and a mission and got no more than a hopeless cause and hate-warped heart. We would lay it all out for them, show how the uncle had framed the boy's outlook and how the boy had been imprisoned within that narrowness, unable, even with the edges of his sharp mind, to pierce the walls of it. We would suggest other places to lay blame, would argue that if just one of our number, one bold, crusading soul of Tykesville, Alabama, had stepped forward, had said, "No, we are not going to leave this boy to be reared by such a man as this," then things could have turned out differently. We would appeal to that common human denominator that tells us we are all a part of some greater and connected design, and that no one stands apart from history and environment, and that when we judge a boy and condemn a boy, we are judging and condemning that history and that environment that gave him birth. Then we would ask for mercy, plead for mercy, beg for mercy. We would be a persuasive team, the young lawyer spilling with zeal and emotion, then the venerable old man coming along afterward, cleaning up the excesses, spinning the facts one last turn with reason and experience and temperance. Yes, we would be persuasive. And we would lose—Macky would almost certainly be sentenced to death.

I told young Marris just that as we left the courthouse that Friday. He didn't answer, just nodded, a reserved sort of separateness in his bearing. I could tell he was beaten: from exhaustion, from self-examination and second-guessing, from wondering whether we'd done enough or whether we could ever do enough to save the life of Royce Macky. And from trying to suppress that question that must have been erupting from his nether-ego: *Why are we doing this and why does it even matter?* We would see each other Monday, I said as I let him go, watched him retreat into his own adaptation of the American dream: a toddling son, a pregnant wife, a small, over-mortgaged house, a promising future. I felt a surge of envy as I walked to my car to drive the six blocks to my own childless house—my wifeless house. A cold place to wait for another Monday morning.

I sat at Melanie's piano, the dusk falling hard around me, staring through my bourbon glass at the tintype of my great-grandfather while I fumbled through the *Moonlight Sonata*. My ear remembered the images, her delicate and certain hands, the way they would stretch like artful bridges over the keys, how the music would emerge so round and so long and so perfect, her eyes shut on all of space and time, her head canted just so, pouring herself through the instrument, and the instrument responding under her all-feeling hands, absorbing the fluidity of her passion and channeling it from keys to humming strings, filling the room with her sagacious grace, until the amazed timbers and joists took up the sound, and the music came suddenly from everywhere and nowhere, as if the house itself had become an extension of the instrument.

I reached for my whisky and left my own crude rendition of Beethoven to dissolve in a half-rendered mire of mournful, disharmonic echoes. The old house was bloated with oppressive redolence. To the east, a porcelain pitcher and we were standing on Pont Neuf, watching the tourist barges ply the Seine, waving back to the happy faces cruising beneath us. Then west and the baroque brass candlesticks and we were in that Istanbul bazaar, moving among the crowd and the air charged with the sea and the aromas of exotic spices, while the chant of a muezzin wended through the golden twilight. Thirty-six years of marriage keep hard memories, leave vast pits of emptiness for a sardonic widower to negotiate. So the bourbon needs to be good, needs to be clear-looking and pleasing to the eye, needs to be bold enough to swallow the memories and the emptiness. I poured a fourth glass, no ice this time.

"What is it that makes you call a thing evil, anyway?" Where did he hear such a question as that? How did he know to ask it of me? The issue seems a facile one on the surface. But only on the surface. *I know it is evil because . . . because it's . . . because it seems to be so.* And why does it seem to be so? *Because murder is harmful. Because taking life is wrong.* And why is taking life wrong and murder harmful? There is surely no historical precedent to support such a hypothesis. Just follow any trail of blood back far enough and you'll find human nature at the source of it. *But there are some circumstances that justify taking life, situations where violence is necessary, where killing produces desirable results.* My point exactly. *But I didn't come here to discuss your odious philosophy.* So walk away. Just walk away.

But walk away where? There is no more sanctuary. Life has unspooled me into a straightjacket of meaningless choices. Compass points drift against a featureless horizon—north, south, east and west are mere provisional constructs, anchorless and without the substance of underlying certainty. The skulls of Chele Kula spin around me like numbers on a roulette wheel, 952 whirring, random points, and where it stops, pure and fantastic chance.

Who were these people anyway, these Serbian rebels, suckered into slaughter for a cause and a glory now so absurdly reduced to historical trivia? What is it that makes you call a thing evil? I used to know, but now I've forgotten. I used to think I knew, but maybe I never did, because maybe what makes you call a thing evil is something apart from evil itself. Because maybe evil itself, if it even exists, can never be pinned down, can never be fixed upon any more than a drifting compass point or the random spinning of a wheel of numbers. Apprehension amends reality and nothing but death is irrevocable and nothing is immutable. So what does one make of those masons who trowelled their enemy's skulls into that tower wall that future voyeurs might look upon their handiwork and call it glorious or not call it glorious, or call it evil or not call it evil, and what polestar is there to gauge who called it right and who called it wrong? I used to know, but now I've forgotten. Now I have forgotten.

Young Marris was displaying that annoying habit of his, holding a pen cap between his teeth while inking down some frenetic memo. Macky sat between us, calm and sphinx-like. Bridgeport was burnishing his case, making his final plea for capital justice. "Never in the history of our county has a deed cried out louder for the ultimate punishment," he told the jury. "Open your souls and hear its cry. Hear the echoes of Jamal Manderson's cry. Hear those cries, ladies and gentlemen. Hear them and heed them." Then turning theatrically, pointing directly into the unflappable face of our client, "Give that man the electric chair!" And then the slow walk back to his table while the silence took on an ominous shape, and time seemed to decelerate, as if in deference to the gravity and depth of the quiet.

Kevin did his part well, a bit too much of his youthful hyperbole coming through in places, but all in all, a professional, well-constructed argument. I should have left it at that, should have thanked the jury, maybe made one last plea for mercy and sat down. But I was latched to some vague notion of duty that required more of me than a token performance. So I rose, walked to that single point of intersection, a dozen pairs of pondering eyes bringing me into focus. As I weighed and considered, my prepared remarks ebbed from memory and I felt as though I were standing on the rim of a great abyss, yet I had never before felt so free as I did at that moment. I turned to my left, where the State's evidence had been gathered: the rope, still made into a noose, a bowie knife smeared with Manderson's blood, an axe and a shotgun taken from the back seat of Macky's car.

"Ladies and gentlemen," I began. "Let us talk for a moment about the fate of Royce Macky." I leaned toward a demure woman on the front row of the jury box, a lady I recognized as the mother of a homely girl who once took piano lessons from Melanie. "Are you ready to discuss it with me, Mrs. Jefferson?" I asked. There followed an edgy moment of speechlessness. "No?" I continued. "Then what about you, Mr. Langston?" I said to the bow-tied gentleman seated next to her. Their startled faces amused me and I couldn't avoid a slight chuckle. Carlton was sitting on the bench, dumbstruck, not believing what he was hearing, but not daring to stop me. Anyone else he would have quickly cut off, but I carried a lot of currency in his courtroom—enough to buy a good deal of latitude. "And what about the rest of you?" I went on. "Is there no one who will discuss Royce Macky's fate with me? No? Not one of you will talk with me about it?" I paused, turned and walked toward the collection of State exhibits. "Well, if none of you want to talk about it," I shouted, "then how in the name of God are we ever going to get anywhere with this trial?"

"Your Honor!" Bridgeport sprung to his feet. "This is highly irregular."

"Highly irregular indeed," I shouted over Carlton's banging gavel.

"Mr. Tarver," Carlton said, dropping his gavel. "I don't know what you're up to, but please just make your argument and do not attempt to converse with the jury."

"I'm sorry, Judge," I said. "May I continue now?"

"Please do."

I cleared my throat silently. "Highly irregular?" I said, looking back at the jury. "I wonder what he meant by that. What is irregular? What is regular? Do you have any idea, Mrs. Jefferson?"

"Bass!" came the cry from the bench.

"Let's look at it this way," I said, picking up the axe

from the pile of exhibits. "Let's say that table there is the whole universe." I walked toward the table where Marris and Macky sat. They scurried backward in their chairs like startled children.

"Stop it right there, Bass," Carlton yelled.

"Let's pretend that table there is the whole wide universe," I continued, undeterred. "Half of it's good and half of it's evil. And let's pretend I'm God." I could hear the scrambling now, the deputies circling about me, uncertain of how to commence the attack. I raised the axe and brought it down on the tabletop. Then twice more and God had finished his work, and the rent table fell to the floor in an open *V*. "Now then," I said. "Now then, Mr. Langston. Mrs. Jefferson. Anyone. Which is the good side and which is the bad side? Who of you can tell the difference? Step forward now, if you can."

The first blow came from behind me, one of the younger deputies, then the others following, wresting the axe from my grip, taking me to the floor amid the chaos and disbelieving gasps. They made short work of cuffing me, even with Marris there alongside, telling them it wasn't necessary, entreating them to let me go and that he would take care of everything. Carlton was off the bench, he and the bailiff ushering the astonished jurors to safety. When they lifted me up, I came eye to eye with Jamal Manderson's mother. Her face was a stoic carving, a judgment-free tabernacle of serenity, enduring within an absurd and furious landscape. I searched her eyes for that infinite reflection, for that diminishing trail of mirrors that led to a place I once thought I knew. I strained and tilted, trying for just the right angle, but there was an opaque veneer over her irises that denied me what I sought, as if she had seen the end of that trail and knew what was there and would keep it, would refuse me entry and leave me ignorant and guessing and struggling and wondering.

They pushed me toward the door, young Marris's voice trilling behind us, dragged me past the fallen-chinned assemblage of clerks and office workers and reporters, then outside where the maizey sunlight blinded and disoriented me and I felt as if space had collapsed around me and that time was moving sideways. It was then I heard the bells, the chiming of the Methodist carillon from across the square, a melodic progression of riffs and echoes followed by twelve intrepid gongs, each one attempting, in its futile way, to pin down time and take its measurement. I counted them all, a dozen bulky, dissonant tones, as they vibrated one by one through the square. And then I waited for the silence, that soundless reassurance that would descend as the twelfth bell faded. But then came another. And another behind that. The deputies paused. The children jumping rope and the old men smoking on their benches and the pert-breasted mothers pushing strollers all paused, all looked about bemusedly as the gongs continued, a new one coming behind the last, each more hideous and mocking than the one before, each one taking us farther away from the comforting certainty of noon.

# Clyde and Jake

Clyde Stearns staggered across the porch, lurched first one way and then the next, finally found balance against the rusted-over washing machine, the same one that had sat there in the same spot where the Haygood Hardware boy had left it ten years ago when he'd brought the new one. The Alabama dusk was settling empty as a desert. Nothing to his left or right but the familiar dirt road winding through the leafless hardwoods, nothing before him but the past, if the past even counted. And behind him where he'd left it, his brother's ghost—Jake's ghost—there at the kitchen table, the feckless face suspended in the feckless air, and he'd turned and walked out defiantly because damned if he was going to take any more haunting from Jake Stearns's ghost so long as he had two good legs beneath him and a full moon on the rise and a fine dirt road to walk on.

They had been loggers, he and Jake, cut timber together for thirty years and more, living under the same roof the better part of that time, during the times when Jake would get his fill of Hilda Townly and storm off vowing she could rot in hell before he'd ever come back, or (more likely) when Hilda would change the locks and leave his clothes and boots and cigarettes in an unceremonious heap on the front stoop. Nine months ago, Hilda had become the agent of her own widowhood—or non-widowhood, more accurately, given they'd never married—when she'd shot Jake through the left eye with a Colt revolver. Now it was just Clyde, logging with any man he could round up with a working chainsaw and a need for a few dollars, and he'd kept at it like that, not as steady as with Jake, but he'd kept at it, except when he'd taken off a week to watch twelve fellow Bedford County citizens find that Hilda Townly had acted in self-defense.

Half a mile along, he felt the headlights against his back and stepped aside to let the pickup pass. But the truck didn't pass. It stopped beside him and he watched as the window rolled down and Vance Densmore's face appeared.

"Where you going, Clyde?" He had to pause to think about it. The dust from the truck tires thickened the air around him and he coughed into his hand as he studied Densmore.

"I said where you going?" Densmore repeated. "You ain't broke down, have you?"

Clyde approached the truck tentatively, leaned in the window and looked around the cab as if he might have left something there. "I'm going to see old man Moats," he said.

"Carlisle Moats? What'a you need with Carlisle Moats? You ain't in trouble, are you?"

Clyde spat out a cord of tobacco juice. "Gonna kill him."

Densmore reached across the seat and opened the door. "Get in the damn truck, Clyde," he ordered.

Vance Densmore had little time to spare between selling cars at his Ford dealership and being a deacon at the Bedford First Baptist Church or president of the Chamber of Commerce or secretary of the Rotary Club or treasurer of the Quarterback Club. But he found time to bring Clyde back to his office at the Ford place and give him a Coke and sit him down across the desk like a customer he was about to finance.

"Clyde, you ain't gonna kill Carlisle Moats," he said. "Now get that idea right outta your head."

"You don't know what I'm gonna do," Clyde said, looking at the floor. "You don't know how it is. He's done come again. Just keeps after me."

"Who's come again?"

"Never mind."

"Who's come again, I said?"

Clyde lifted his eyes to the plaques and certificates papering the wall. Superior Service Award, 1989, Southeastern Dealership of the Year, 1990.

"Listen to me, Clyde," Densmore continued. "Moats was just doing his job. It ain't his fault Hilda got off. It was the jury and the law let her go. I don't like the crazy old bastard any more than you, but blaming him ain't—"

"Was him that charged that jury with all his lies. All them lies about Jake and what they said he done to that woman. That witch. Them jurors only done what they done because of his lies."

"That's the way the law works, Clyde. Moats just argued his client's case like he was paid to do. It's for the jury to decide who's telling the truth. Now they've acted and it's over. You got to get past it."

"Charged 'em full o' lies is what he done. How can they decide the truth when he charged 'em full o' lies?"

Densmore got Clyde another Coke, but he didn't drink any of it. They sat there talking until Clyde's distemper ebbed toward a more agreeable humor and then Densmore ushered him back into the pickup and drove him home, Clyde sitting in sullen contemplation as occasional nightbugs thumped against the windshield. When they reached the house, Densmore aimed his headlights against the front door until Clyde got inside and turned on a few houselights. He left them burning all night.

For two days after that, he rambled from room to room to no good purpose. He didn't see the apparition, but he felt it—sensed its ghostly odor in the kitchen, a sweet, redolent scent, and a wispy voice, not in his ear exactly, but somewhere deeper, urging him on, urging him to do something, even if it wasn't clear what it was that ought to be done.

On the third morning he climbed into the logging truck and rattled off through a thick fog to the unpaved streets of Yellowtown Quarters, driving between the small paintless houses, shotgun houses teetering on cinder block piers with dogs roaming freely beneath them, and woodsmoke curling from stone chimneys, wending aimlessly into the gunmetal sky. Curious faces watched from smoky windows as the truck crept past. He stopped in front of Repton's house and went to the door, left the truck chugging, the diesel belching out plumes of blackness.

Repton met him at the threshold, a hulk of rough ebony with a logger's arms and a face as stony as any pagan god's. Two children peered out from behind his legs. "You wantin' to work today?" Clyde asked. Repton turned back inside without speaking, left the door open though the morning air was frigid. The children hurried after him, glancing back timidly at Clyde. He heard Repton's voice from the next room, then that of a woman, but he couldn't make out the words. The air smelled of chicory and frying sausage. In a moment Repton returned carrying a tattered wool overshirt and a chainsaw. By eight-thirty, they were in the woods.

They cut all morning and well into the afternoon before they broke. Sitting in the truck with the doors open, they ate the ham sandwiches from the paper sack that Clyde had brought and a can of sardines that Repton contributed. They were miles off the paved road, and the only sounds besides their own voices were the wind through the treetops and the occasional bleating of a hawk. Clyde chewed on a sardine as he looked out through the cracked windshield. "You believe in ghosts?" he asked.

Repton paused to consider. "Why you ask?"

"Cause I wanna know, goddamn it. That's why I asked."

Repton scratched his sideburn. "Ain't never seen nare ghost myself," he said. "But Lilly, she say she seen 'em before. Seen her mama coming cross that field behind our house. But me, I ain't never seen nare one."

"You believe Lilly?"

Repton swallowed a bite of his sandwich. "I reckon if she say she seen it, then she sho'nough did see it."

Clyde thought this over as he chewed. "Did it talk to her?"

"I can't say as I recall her saying."

"You think a ghost can talk to a man?"

"If a ghost *wanna* talk to a man, then I reckon it can."

Clyde finished his sandwich, pulled a grease rag from his hip pocket and wiped his mouth. He looked at Repton. "If a ghost told you to do something, would you do it?"

Repton looked away thoughtfully. "I guess that gone depend on what the ghost tell me to do."

"What if it told you to kill somebody?"

Repton shot Clyde a sober glance. "Then I'd sho' think that over mighty careful. A ghost like that liable to been sent round by the Devil."

"But how you supposed to know?" Clyde pounded his fist to the steering wheel. "How can you tell where it come from?"

Repton shifted sideways in his seat, leaned back against the door. "Whose ghost been haunting you, Clyde?"

Clyde looked down. "None of your goddamn business."

Repton shrugged. "I just wondered."

"No goddamn ghost been'a haunting Clyde Stearns. I ain't gonna be haunted by no ghost."

"I just wondered, is all."

Clyde inhaled, composed himself. "But if a ghost ain't from hell . . . if a ghost ain't sent by the Devil, then don't that mean it's due to be respected?"

"You way beyond me now, Clyde Stearns."

"If it ain't sent by the Devil, then ain't a body obliged to listen to it? To do what it says?"

Repton took a toothpick from his shirt pocket and put it in his mouth. "I ain't qualified to answer that. You need to go to yo preacher with that."

Clyde turned. His eyes were flickering and there was an almost tactile aura of energy about him that seemed to spring at once from everywhere and nowhere, twisting around his head like a scarf. "If I make it not to be the Devil's messenger, then I don't see how it can be otherwise than a Commandment for me to follow. It can't be nothing less than a Commandment."

"You letting yo senses run off without you, Clyde. You best slow down and consider."

Clyde didn't answer, just stared through the windshield, the aura fading now. He brushed the empty lunchsack out the door and reached for his Redman pouch. "I'm done cutting for today," he said. "I got to see a man this evening on some other business."

"What you talking 'bout, Clyde? Who you got to see?"

Clyde slammed the door shut and tried the ignition. "Carlisle Moats," he said.

"*Carlisle Moats*? You ain't got no business with Carlisle Moats. You need to keep fur away from him."

The engine caught on the third try. "I'll pick you up at eight tomorrow. We oughta finish by early afternoon."

"You keep yourself away from Carlisle Moats, you hear. You done took leave of yo better senses, talking 'bout ghosts and killing somebody and going to see Carlisle Moats." Clyde popped the clutch and Repton had to hang on to keep from falling out of the cab. He slammed his door just ahead of an approaching sweetgum sapling as they bounded down the logging road, Clyde's hands locked over the wheel, Repton bracing himself against the dash.

Time and distance flowed by in a seamless wash of timber and dust and impermeable gray sky. They entered Yellowtown Quarters, stopped before the house without paint or skirting, where dogs moved like smoke among the piers and the two immutable faces watched through the single front window. Repton took his saw and disappeared and Clyde pulled the truck forward, worked through the low gears, the truck easing along as slow as the afternoon light. Then sudden as thunder, a young boy on a bicycle, and Clyde was slamming his feet against clutch and brake, the truck groaning to a stop just in time, and then a second boy, older, sudden as the first, the massive rock in his cocked, relentless hand, running hard until the hand was empty and the bicycle on the ground and the younger boy sprawled beside it. Clyde got down from the cab and came around to face the older youth, the fallen boy and bicycle in the dirt between them, the fierce, unrepentant eyes of the attacker locked to his own and the voice detached, cool and passionless. "Hiss mine. Fucka stole it." He walked to the bike and uprighted it, cursorily inspected it. "Fucka stole it," he repeated, then got on the bike and rode away.

Clyde knelt beside the downed boy. With a shaky hand, he reached for the gash where the blood spread out over the sepia skin. The boy jerked as if sensing the approaching touch, looked up at Clyde with the gaping eyes of guilt.

"You okay?" Clyde asked.

The boy gathered himself on unsure legs, his eyes vast as oceans. He backed off a few steps, then turned and ran away. Clyde watched him disappear into one of the houses. Then he looked down and saw the blood on the ground, even thought he could smell it.

He got back in his truck. It was late afternoon and the sky was thick with the grayness of spoiled beef. The nearly obliterated sun winked sickly through the overcast heavens like a woozy, bloated eye. He drove by instinct and without thought of destination, drove until he knew without reflection or understanding where he would go.

He parked the truck on the main road beside the driveway to Moats's farm and took the pistol from under the seat and pocketed it. The two hundred yards of driveway was lined with brush and overgrowth and canopied by low-hanging limbs. At the end of the driveway was Moats's Lincoln, and beyond that, the farmhouse, a dilapidated assemblage of decaying wood surrounded by waist-high weeds and arthritic shrubs. He waded through the weeds and banged against the door and waited for an answer. None came. He tried the door, found it locked, then he heard the shooting.

He walked around back toward the sound, fingering the pistol in his pocket. Moats sat in a lawn chair among the weeds, his back to Clyde, a pistol held at arm's length. Locks of thinning gray hair trailed down to his shoulders, weakly blanketing the scaly crown of his head. On a table beside him was a pint canning-jar half full of amber liquid, and beside that, an open fifth of Maker's Mark. Fifty feet beyond him, a row of glass bottles rested on stumps. Moats fired the pistol again and one of the bottles exploded. Then he put down the gun and picked up the jar and drank. He spoke without looking back.

"You gonna stand there looking at me or you gonna come around and say hello?"

Clyde froze in mute contemplation.

"Goddamn it, Stearns, I asked you a question." He took up the pistol again, still not looking back, and fired. Another bottle burst.

Clyde stepped toward him. The wind carried the odor of gunpowder through the yard, and the odor spun in his head as he came forward. He tried to make sense of the landscape, the old man in his chair among the weeds, the bottles resting on their stumps, and beyond that, thickets of brambles consuming a tattered, barbed-wire fence and vine-choked fence posts topped with ivory-colored caps, then the horizon itself, an infinite abyss of primal darkness that seemed to swallow all light save for a few dim rays of gray that seeped through as if the abyss intended it, so that one might mark its emptiness against some scant sliver of radiance.

"I didn't come to say hello," said Clyde.

"You came to question me then." Moats set the pistol on the table and turned. "About your brother's case, I reckon. Come around here and sit where I can see you."

Clyde came forward and took a seat on a willow stump so that he looked upon Moats's profile. Moats picked up the jar and lifted it to his mouth. "There ain't nothing to question," Clyde said. "I heard you charge that jury. Heard your lies about Jake."

Moats smiled. His head was a rounded-edged square of ancient, superfluous flesh. A radish-like abscess on his chin oozed a sappy plasma. His eyes were as clear as spring-water.

"You heard them and you've thought about them ever since," said Moats. "And what good has all your reflection done you?"

Clyde looked beyond the bottles to the fence posts, tried to make out the shapes of the white caps atop the posts. "Ain't done a bit of good. Thinking on it don't help."

"Indeed. Reflection is of no value. A trick of the mind to anguish the soul."

Clyde reached in his pocket and felt the pistol. "You go around lying for money. It ain't right and I intend to set it straight."

"You're right that I do it for money, Stearns. But you're wrong about it being a lie. You see son, there ain't no lies and there ain't no truth. They're both illusions. There's one side of a story and then there's the other side, and it's the best argued side that survives as what folks call the truth. But that ain't really the truth, you understand. Just the illusion of truth."

"You got a mouthful of fancy words, ain't you?"

Moats laughed, picked up the gun from the table and aimed it at a bottle. Clyde tightened the grip on his own weapon. "So you ran off from that trial and been stewing ever since about what that jury did, and all along it ain't nothing but your own thinking about it that's got you so poisoned inside." He fired and another bottle exploded.

"I come here to do more than think on it," said Clyde.

"That so?" asked Moats, turning to him. "What are you gonna do then?"

"I'm gonna kill you to start with."

Moats put down the gun and picked up the jar. He drained the last of the whisky, picked up the bottle and refilled the jar and handed it to Clyde. "Take a drink of that, boy," he said.

"I don't want none," said Clyde.

"If you wanna avenge your brother, you're going about it all wrong. You can kill me dead as T-bone steak and what've you done? You'll go back home and keep thinking, keep reflecting, keep stewing." He drank from the jar and offered it again to Clyde. "Take a drink of this. It'll do you more good than that pistol in your pocket ever will."

Clyde took the jar, looked down into the gold liquid as the fumes spread upward through his head. "What's it take then?" he asked. "What's it take to set something right?"

"You can't. Right and wrong, they're both the same thing. Illusions. You can't set things right 'cause there *ain't* no right. What's right today is wrong tomorrow and vice versa. Might as well accept it that way because you can't change it. All you can do is alter the way you look at the world. Go ahead and take a drink of that."

Clyde brought the jar to his mouth and gulped down a harsh swallow, coughed and spit as he passed the jar back to Moats. "It's like going to the picture show," Moats continued. "You sit on the back row and you see it one way. Sit down front and you see it another way. But it's the same picture. Moving about don't change the picture, it just changes how you look at the picture. Same it is with life. Nothing you do changes it. Nothing you do matters. All you can do is alter how you look at it." Moats drank from the jar, wiped his mouth on his sleeve and handed it back to Clyde.

"That don't seem a sensible way to look at things," Clyde said.

"No?"

"If I kill you, that'll matter a lot."

"Will it?" said Moats. "How?"

Clyde took another drink. "You wouldn't be in the picture no more."

A deep laugh spiraled up from Moats's belly and twisted into the night, a primitive helix of dark energy, mocking of hope and reason. His eyes sparked. "So you would change the picture just like the projector man changes a reel of film. But you'd soon find that the new film was no different. Maybe it has different characters, maybe the plot's changed, but the outcome is always the same. In the end, it's all an illusion. Nothing matters."

Clyde considered his words, searched his head for some reply. "You talk too goddamn much," he said.

"Face it son. Nothing matters. Not you, not me, not Jake. Our destinies are already written by one grand law of the universe: The strongest and fittest survive. The strongest species, the strongest ideas, the strongest arguments. Nothing can change that and nothing else matters."

Clyde turned up the jar and felt the liquor moving through his head. He set the jar down hard and looked toward the fence, squinting the distance into focus. Though the light had faded, he could make out a few details of the objects atop the fence posts. They were like white orbs pocked with dark hollows and as he stared at them, the markings began to resolve into the outlines of sockets—eyes and noses such as those of human skulls. He fixed on one of the ossified faces, his senses suspended in abeyance. Then it appeared before him as it had in the kitchen, the vapid countenance floating directly before the skull, its features amorphous and fluid and with darkness surrounding it. He searched the form for Jake's eyes, for his brother's mouth, for the familiar crop of hair, listened for the voice that had chided him time and again, waiting to accept his final chastisement. But the form was unstable, changing like the ropes of light at the bottom of a clear pool until only gradually could he begin to discern its features, and as he examined the apparition, he realized that he was not looking upon the face of his brother at all, but at an entirely different face, and as the details clarified, he saw in the image his own reflection, his own eyes and nose and hair, hovering like an illusion before the skull. He sat there on the willow stump transfixed, the canning-jar in his hand, unable to move, unable to look away until at last the explosion came and the skull splintered into a thousand bony slivers. He turned and looked at Moats, the smoking pistol extended before him, a sardonic smile on his face, and he could feel the clear blue eyes of the old man plundering his insides.

He got up without a word and walked out to the main road and got in his truck. The cold had grown thick and the darkness was now complete and the sky without reference of moon or stars. He heard the words of Moats rewinding through his head, *everything is illusion, nothing matters,* and he tried to fit the words with all he knew and understood and the words would not fit, but neither would they leave him alone.

He drove west toward the Bogahatchee River and the night air blew through the truck in frigid bursts, but he did not feel its icy bite. He stopped at the Tyson-Storey Bridge. The road was empty and he got out and walked to the edge of the bank. He couldn't see the river, but he heard the rushing current far below, and the sounds of the water melded with the voice of Carlisle Moats in a mnemonic rhyme. *Everything is illusion. Nothing matters.*

He got back into the truck and took off the brake and let it roll onto the shoulder of the road. As it coasted forward, he sensed a presence to his right and he looked and saw Jake leaning back in the seat, an expression of sublime contentment on his face, his smile so carefree it was as though they were boys again when the two of them had no fears of the future and no regrets of the past and the moment was all there was.

The truck gained momentum, bumping along the shoulder, veering farther off the road on a downward incline. Clyde felt his spirit rising as he watched Jake. He wanted to take him in his arms, to tell him it was all right, that vengeance was an illusion and that nothing mattered except how you looked at things or what seat in the picture show you chose, but as he regarded the virgin peacefulness on Jake's face, he knew that it was unnecessary.

The truck lurched forward, bouncing Clyde's head against the wheel. He started as if suddenly awakened from a nightmare, grabbed for the door handle and began to wrestle with it. Brushes and tree limbs slashed through the open window as he struggled with the jammed latch. He felt the truck accelerating and tipping toward vertical and the liquid fear of rushing adrenaline surged through his chest. He braced his foot against the floorboard hump and shoved against the door with all his strength. As it sprung open, he dived out into the night. He floated at first, experienced the sheer weightlessness of his body, then tumbled through trees and brush and boulders with no awareness of direction. Finally, he heard the sound of the river and Moats's words mingled with the rushing water and he used the sound to orient himself. He grabbed at the brushes and limbs flying past him, slowing his descent until finally he tumbled to rest on a narrow ledge with a firm branch to hold to. The log truck plunged ahead of him, knifing downward in a vertical dive, the cab pulling the trailer behind it through its freefall. The rig hit the water and exploded into a fireball that lit the night in a burst of orange, then died away like a fading flare as the river swallowed the fire.

Clyde pulled himself to his feet, gathering, little by little, his balance and orientation. He turned his eyes upward and noticed that the moon had come out and was shimmering above him like a liquid silver dollar. Carefully, he began to climb, using the milky light to search out the best footholds, taking special caution that his steps found firm and trustworthy earth as he scouted for the best path up the embankment.

## Playing Bingo for Money

Choices.

My life is beset with choices. To be or not to be. Straight up or on the rocks. Paper or plastic. Beset, befuddled, bedeviled, becudgeled, besmothered, beslobbered . . . *bethumped* . . . with choices. Choices bedamned, my inner voice bemoans as I enter the parking deck in my Buick LeSabre. The attendant approaches menacingly. I can feel him wielding more choices.

"Gone be leaving before noon or staying all day?"

I freeze momentarily, considering how to respond to this either-or. My mind shuffles the options. I am headed for the Bedford County Courthouse to try—or to try to settle—the case of Aggie Bingo vs. Holston Trucking Company. Five other cases are set on this morning's docket. Which will the judge call first? If not Aggie's, will he send us away until another day? And there is still the possibility of the oft-maligned courthouse-steps settlement. I could bedone and begone by ten o'clock. But if we start the trial, I'll be here all day. I concoct an ingenious reply, craftily weaving all possibilities into one succinct response that I deliver with casual aplomb.

"Depends."

The attendant's eyes roll backward until I am looking into two globules of eggshell putty. He is either expressing, with theatrical sarcasm, his exasperation with my refusal to choose or experiencing a grand mal seizure. I am hoping for the seizure. Ahh, but the irises reappear.

"Park over between that Lexus and the green Bronco."

He has deliberately assigned me to the narrowest space in the entire deck, one into which my LeSabre cannot possibly fit and still allow room for my exit. I resolve not to accept such shabby treatment from the likes of a parking lot attendant. I am, after all, a lawyer and I don't have to take this belittlement. I know how to forcefully assert my rights.

"Isn't that space a little small for my car?"

"You got room. Pull on in."

I mumble a caustic curse and obey. One must sometimes reserve one's energies in quarrels of this sort. Wisdom and discretion often require the swallowing of pride in order that vital piss and vinegar are not needlessly bespattered upon immaterial conflict. Resolving to conserve my verve for the impending strife of the courtroom, I pull sheepishly into the constricted space, a blood clot entering a clogged artery. I gently open the LeSabre door, being extraordinarily careful not to allow it to touch the luscious, glossy blackness of the virgin Lexus. With my door carefully positioned at its apogee, oversized briefcase in my lap, I gingerly set one foot to the pavement and prepare to stand. Employing all of the coordination and grace of Michael Jordan gliding under the basket for a reverse slam dunk, I catapult myself upward, slamming my chest into the door and sending it crashing into the Lexus at which point it ping-pongs back like a one ton hammer crushing my shin against the LeSabre, at which point I quite naturally grab my shin with both hands, dropping my briefcase on my foot and yell *"SHIT!"* inadvertently striking the door again, with my shoulder this time, and propelling it smartly back for a second violent encounter with the freshly mangled black paint of the Lexus.

"Sssheeeit man! What you trying to do?" the attendant politely inquires.

"Tight space you put me in here sport," I gasp, holding my throbbing shin and checking for broken bones.

"Sssheeeit man!" he sibilates, noticeably unconcerned for my own well-being. "Look what you done to that car."

Controlling my mounting anger at his insensitivity to my searing pain, I astutely conclude that I must quickly defuse this situation. Always thinking like a lawyer, I ingeniously formulate a single rhetorical question that will instantly assuage all of his concerns.

"Ain't *your* car is it?"

His eyes roll backward again as I lock the LeSabre and hobble toward the street. Is it the seizure this time? Apparently not, as I hear his beguiling voice singing in the background.

"I'm telling who done this."

I wave goodbye, choosing not to look back, and thinking what a wonderful start this day has gotten off to. Aggie Bingo is beriddled with luck to have me as her champion.

$$$

Entering the courthouse, I queue up behind an eclectic mix of Bedford County citizens, each awaiting their turn to pass under the official Bedford County Metal Detector, a contraption I have detested from the first day the county installed it and have grown to hate even more with each pass I make through its meddlesome threshold. No one can remember the last time a terrorist or a postal worker smuggled a Thompson into the building and wasted a few lawyers and clerks or a judge or two. Nevertheless, the County Commission, in its infinite wisdom (as is oft said of politicians), decided to take preemptive action lest some Jihad warrior decide that Bedford County, Alabama, would be the perfect place to advance his agenda by taking out a few local citizens and maybe, on a good day, even a couple of big-shot lawyers from Montgomery or Birmingham. Hence, the official Bedford County Metal Detector. I know of other counties where they have these things and they always let the lawyers walk right on around them. No special favors here though. In the eyes of the Bedford County Sheriff's Department, we are all potential Jihad postal workers.

No sooner do I step through the annoying monstrosity than it erupts with a series of sharp beeps and flashing lights, identifying me as a possible mass murderer. Three khaki-clad deputies look on lazily. If I were a postal worker, I could be on the third floor before they stirred.

"Step over here, please," the buxom, blond female of the crew finally orders. One of her overweight colleagues leans against a table and looks on amusedly while he works over a stick of gum, a full one-half of his corpulent ass spread over the tabletop. The uniformed blond comes at me with what looks like an electric charcoal starter and begins probing my personal space. As the probe passes near my genitalia, an alarm goes off.

"Must be that old blue steel," I crack and give her a quick wink. She acts as though she is not amused, but I know she is only acting. The chubby one, however, is laughing from deep in his belly, dangling a stout leg from the table while I disgorge the contents of my pockets.

"Just a false positive," she says dryly. "Nothing dangerous in *these* pants." She looks at me as if to say *gotcha*. Chubby begins to laugh louder, the insubstantial tabletop now undulating beneath the pulse of his jovial buttock.

After concluding that my belt buckle is the source of all this merriment, the deputies allow me to pass. As I walk away, I consider whether it might be worth sacrificing a few lawyers, clerks, and judges once every eon or so in order to be rid of that goddamn thing. Before I am out of earshot, I hear it again: *beep, beep, beep* . . . . "Step over here, please." Ahh, to live in such times as these.

$$$

The trial of Bingo vs. Holston Trucking is to be held in the second-floor courtroom of the Honorable J. Cavandar Prickle. The Honorable J. Cavandar Prickle has been on the bench a little less than a year, having replaced one of the great jurists in the history of Bedford County, the Honorable Penrose Samuels, affectionately known to the Bedford County bar as Drinkin' Sammy. The difference between the two is like day and night or, as Drinkin' Sammy would have said, God rest his soul, the forces of darkness and the power of enlightenment. Drinkin' Sammy was from an old blue-blooded Bedford County family whose pedigree could be traced back to the earliest settlers of Alabama. A Harvard-educated man, Drinkin' Sammy could quote Shakespeare and scripture all day long and spout off more Latin phrases than a Black's Law Dictionary. He was a man of the people—a judge dedicated to the proposition that no citizen of Bedford County was ever going to sit on the back seat of the bus of justice whenever it rolled through his courtroom. This proved to be a quite pertinent axiom in cases that pitted one of our beloved locals against an out-of-state insurance company. Drinkin' Sammy's devotion to this particular principle got him into nasty flame wars with some of the hotshot firms in Montgomery and Birmingham who regularly invaded his fiefdom for the sole and sinister purpose of abetting their insurance company clients in denying payment of the honest claims of local residents, the terms "honest" and "local" being synonymous and interchangeable in this context. These disputes often turned vicious and resulted in the spreading of much malicious gossip about Drinkin' Sammy, not to mention several investigations by the state bar. The saddest thing about it all was that the cirrhosis got him before he could clear his name once and for good. Drinkin' Sammy may be gone, but he will never be forgotten. I'll never be able to go into his old courtroom without imagining him up there on his bench in his flowing black robe, peering out innocently from behind the jet-black sunglasses, the two days' growth of facial hair casting a dignified shadow over his countenance. He was, let it be said, the very personification of justice.

His replacement (and I hesitate even to use the word) is, to be objective about it, an inexperienced, smooth-faced, blond-haired, wet-behind-the-ears, big-moneyed, right-winged, Christian-Coalition-suck-up, plaintiff-hating, egg-sucking, Republican pissant. It is rumored in some circles that the Honorable J. Cavandar Prickle was actually born at the Country Club, but this is obviously untrue and is only repeated by those who do not like him personally. I maintain that he was merely conceived at the Country Club—begotten, as it were, in a sand trap off the eighteenth fairway.

In spite of his many shortcomings, the Honorable J. Cavandar Prickle has his supporters—mainly hotshot insurance defense lawyers, bankers, business executives, and moneyed people who trust him to intervene in the judicial process on their behalf lest a Bedford County jury attempt to redistribute a portion of their wealth to some undeserving crippled, homeless orphan who lost both legs and both parents in a car wreck caused by a drunken insurance executive whose company denies all liability for the accident and, just for good measure, corruptly refuses to pay off on the parents' life-insurance policies. These are the same people who so maliciously pursued Drinkin' Sammy. When Drinkin' Sammy passed on to his reward, they celebrated their good fortune by successfully lobbying the governor for the appointment of the Honorable J. Cavandar Prickle as the first Republican Circuit Judge in the history of Bedford County. Now, things will never be the same. Gone from Drinkin' Sammy's old office are the M. C. Escher prints and the faux marble bust of Mark Twain, blasphemously replaced with a wooden plaque of the Ten Commandments and pictures of Ronald Reagan. It has been a difficult period of transition.

Those of us in the plaintiff's bar have also noticed a disturbing show of familiarity between the insurance defense lawyers who supported the Honorable J. Cavandar Prickle and their hero that we find to be unprofessional and downright tawdry. When court is in session, they politely refer to him as Judge Prickle. But in the halls, when they think no one is watching, they slap him on the back and call him Cav. While this is disturbing to us, we have formulated a responsive strategy that appropriately addresses the problem and makes us feel better in the process of its implementation. When we think no one is watching, we slap each other on the back and call him Judge Prick.

$$$

I limp into the pompous wood-paneled courtroom through huge leather-veneered double doors, my overstuffed briefcase in hand, and immediately begin perusing the myriad faces in search of Aggie's. Ever since the day Horace Applebee missed the call of his case from sleeping off a hangover, I have entered the courtroom on trial day with a nervous apprehension that my client won't show. My mind races madly, bestirred with the possibilities. Did I forget to inform them of the trial date? Is this the right day? Am I in the right courtroom? What century is this?

Luckily for Horace, the judge on his case was Drinkin' Sammy, who was always understanding about such things. He granted me a postponement for "just cause" over the histrionic and vituperative remonstrations of Clyde Morton, a hot-headed, arm-waving runt of a lawyer from Montgomery who represented the supermarket where Horace had slipped on a string bean that had somehow found its way to an aisle in the wine section. Clyde bitched and whined like it was his own money at stake. Then he finally did the noble thing and settled with us for a semi-fair sum "just to keep from having to come back before that whisky-logged son of a bitch." (Clyde was never one to put his faith in diplomacy.) When it came to looking out for the abused victims of corporate callousness, Drinkin' Sammy's heart was as warm as a mother's milk. Not so with Judge Prick though. His heart is as cold as a dead Eskimo.

My anxiety eases as I scout over the courtroom and lock onto Billy Strickland, Aggie's live-in boyfriend. He sits there alone in the pew, the garnet and gold Florida State cap perched belligerently atop his head, the dingy unwashed auburn hair dangling to his collar. He is head-to-toe in faded denim, the jacket concealing the Confederate battle flag, which I know to be tattooed into his lean, hard forearm. His cavernous nostrils are flared wildly, his face besmeared with unhappy wrinkles as if he were holding a fart in his nose.

Billy and I have had somewhat of a falling out since his last conviction for drunk driving. After successfully dodging justice on two prior occasions, with my expert assistance, of course, he finally got nailed. Naturally, he blames me. If only I had done this or that or called this witness or made that objection. Though he basically disgusts me, I resolve to be civil to him today and to greet him with warm friendship. I catch his eye beneath the golden embossment of Chief Osceola's war bonnet that rises aggressively above the bill of the cap.

"Roll Tide, Billy Boy!" I cannot resist a slight jab with the needle.

He mutters something unintelligible. The wrinkles grow angrier.

"Take off that cap in here and try to show a little class. A juror might see you."

More unintelligible grunts as he complies with my suggestion.

"Where's Aggie?"

Again, more garbled muttering.

"Speak up will you!"

"She went to pee!" he shouts. The myriad faces all look around.

I canvass the hall for Aggie, lurking just outside the women's restroom. Nondescript people are milling all about, many of them potential jurors. I have stressed to Aggie the importance of employing all of her manners and grace anytime she enters the courthouse. "The next person you encounter could be on *your jury*," I caution. It does not help to advance the plaintiff's case for the plaintiff to push aside a stumbly old blue-haired woman in order to secure the last spot on an elevator stuffed with potential jurors. And experience has taught that it is damned counterproductive when the lawyer doesn't know about the incident until the client mentions it just after the last juror is struck and the blue-hair is seated on the front row of the jury box, beaming malevolent smiles at the plaintiff and his lawyer. Even Drinkin' Sammy wasn't able to straighten that shit out.

I wait nervously outside the restroom door, nodding smiles at the ladies as they exit. I am concerned about Aggie's appearance. She is, to put it gently, a rather large, roughhewn woman with a penchant for bedraping her ample posterior with insufficient quantities of polyester. But we have discussed this and she has assured me that she will be appropriately attired. As I wait for what seems an inordinately long time, I hear a voice from behind. "Billy said you was looking for me." Turning, I come face-to-face with my client. I gasp. She is standing there in the hall smiling at me, her brontosaurian form teetering precariously on six-inch stiletto heels. As I greet her, my voice rises involuntarily several decibels and an octave.

"What are you *doing* in those goddamn shoes?"

She is initially dumbstruck by my reaction. When she

tries to speak, she tears up. Massive black underscorings of coagulated mascara are in imminent danger of melting. "You . . . you told me to dress nice."

"Aggie! You are here because you sustained a *back injury*. You are supposed to be in *chronic, debilitating pain*. What is the jury going to think when they see you in those . . . those orthopedic nightmares?"

"I . . . I never thought—"

"Get back in the bathroom quick. There's a Payless shoe store two blocks from the courthouse. I'll send Billy after something appropriate. What size do you wear?"

"Either nine-and-a-halfs or tens. Depends on the shoe."

Another choice to be made.

"Get back in there. Don't let anybody that might be on the jury see you."

"How will I know who might be on the jury?"

"How the hell would I know? Just use some common sense for godsakes."

"But how will I know when you're back?"

"I'll send Billy . . . uhhh . . . ." I suddenly realize the problem. "I'll . . . I'll . . . goddammit, I don't know. I'll think of something. Just get in there."

The secret of being a successful plaintiff's lawyer is maintaining one's calm in the face of impending disaster, tending to those unanticipated crises that spring forth from nowhere at the ninth hour and handling them with dignified professionalism and a cool head. Lesser attorneys would have folded their hand on this case long ago. Not me. I'm playing this one out to the last card. I am determined, against mounting odds, to achieve justice for Aggie Bingo.

$$$

After fronting Billy the money for the shoes together with detailed instructions as to what to buy, and setting him on his way to Payless with great trepidation, I reenter the courtroom to assess the situation. And learn, much to my dismay, that young Judge Prick has already called Aggie's case and is in the process of deputizing a *posse comitatus* to go out searching for me. He sits righteously on the bench in his flowing black robe surrounded by a gaggle of lawyers, all paying appropriate homage, all of whom have cases set for trial today. My eyes fix upon the beguiling, redheaded Mildred Mahorne, the Montgomery lawyer hired by Statewide Indemnity to represent Holston Trucking, the corporate bully that so tragically injured Aggie Bingo. Judge Prick sees me enter and immediately beckons me forward for a high-level conference. Wilfred Jacobs, a wiry, crinkled, gray-headed old geezer and veteran of many a courtroom setback, stands by the bench leering out at me through suppressed laughter, his chestnut teeth and liver spots standing out against his pallid skin. There is a glare in young Judge Prick's blue eyes that bespeaks aggression.

"And just *where* have you been?" his prissy voice wants to know. "And just *where* is your client? And are *you* ready to go to trial?"

Which to answer first? More choices.

"Your honor, my client had a minor medical emergency."

"A *minor* medical emergency?" He asks as though my veracity is in question. "And what exactly is a *minor* medical emergency?"

"A problem with her feet, Judge. We're on top of it. We'll be ready to go any minute."

"Well I certainly wouldn't want this court's schedule to inconvenience you in the slightest. Just tell us what time you want to start your case and we'll all try to accommodate you." Sarcasm is an art in which many judges are well practiced. It does not, however, become young Judge Prick.

"Give me twenty minutes, Judge. Then we'll be ready to rock and roll." I can see immediately from the flush in his cheeks that I have miscalculated the amount of time I should have requested.

"*Twenty minutes*?" His youthful composure crumbles like a stale cracker. "You get this case ready to go in five minutes or I'll dismiss it so fast you'll think it was gone yesterday!"

"Five minutes it is, Judge," I concur unruffled, knowing

full well that five minutes in this courtroom is the temporal equivalent of half an hour in real-world time. "We'll be ready to go in *five minutes*."

"Aggie *Bingo*? Seriously, is that her real name?"

"That's it, Judge. The one and only."

"Bingo in five minutes then," Judge Prick declares, smiling at the spontaneity of his wit as he fiddles with his watch stem like a child picking at a scab.

"I never could win nothing at bingo," Wilfred Jacobs wheezes through nicotine-seasoned vocal cords. The gaggle laughs politely in broken unison at this asinine remark. *Or anything else either*, I want to say, but suppress the urge. Discipline is the hallmark of a successful plaintiff's lawyer.

$$$

I sit across the table from Mildred Mahorne, her delectable red hair bouncing with every movement of her head, exposing flashes of the zillion-carat diamond earrings that dangle bewitchingly from her soft lobes. Judge Prick has ordered us into the conference room with instructions to make one final diligent effort to settle this case while he takes up a motion hearing in a matter he deems to be of greater import. So much for the five-minute deadline. Mildred's penetrating blue eyes look out from under the gentle arches of her deep Bordeaux brows. I am hoping that those eyes did not espy Aggie strutting into the courtroom in her chiropractic calamities. But Mildred is practiced in this routine—her eyes reveal nothing. If she did see the shoes, she will spring it on Aggie during cross-examination: "Didn't I see you in different shoes when you came in this morning? And these shoes you have on now, you purchased them just minutes ago? And at the direction of your *LAWYER*? And the spiked heels are *GONE*? And you got rid of them at the direction of your *LAWYER*?" Mildred is a merciless dynamo with a take-no-prisoners mentality. Aggie figures not to fare too well under her withering questioning.

"I'm going to go ahead and put it all on the table,"

declares Mildred convincingly. "Five thousand dollars. That's all the settlement authority I've got. That's all the authority I will ever have for this case. That's all the authority I will *ever ask for* in this case." There is an air of finality in her voice. But I am not persuaded.

"I'll take it to her, but I'm not optimistic she'll accept it. Five thousand doesn't go far when you consider a thousand dollars in chiropractic bills, three thousand in time out of work, and then there's my—"

"Don't even *try* to sell me that shit about lost time out of work," she rudely dares me. "She's never even filed a tax return. And all you've got to back up what she says about lost wages is her deadbeat live-in boyfriend saying she felt too bad to go clean houses for ten dollars an hour for people they can't even remember."

I remain unflappable in the face of this outburst. "It may not be the strongest part of my case. But when the jury hears of the months of agony and suffering she went through because your company's callous driver smashed her Pinto into next week with his ten-ton monster truck—"

"Scratching her rear bumper to the tune of exactly one hundred thirty-seven dollars and twenty-four cents."

"And viciously twisting her spinal cord, leaving her sprained, strained, in spasms—"

"Five thousand dollars is it. Take it or leave it, but don't come asking for more."

"I'll talk to her. But don't get your hopes up."

"*My* hopes are that she'll turn it down. I'd *love* to try this case." She stands to indicate the negotiations are over. Then, almost as an afterthought, she pauses to smile directly into my face, her perfidious eyes twinkling. "Since I'm laying it all on the table anyway, I might as well let you see this." She throws a thick file to the table that hits with a splat. "Take a look."

Even before taking up the file, I know instinctively that this cannot be good for us. My premonition is confirmed in spades as I flip through the folder's contents. Page after page of Aggie Bingo's medical records showing "patient complaining of chronic back pain" or "patient is back for recheck of back problems." A dozen doctors and clinics, all treating the same complaints. And all dated *before* the wreck with Holston Trucking. While this evidence would be devastating enough standing alone, its effect is compounded by Aggie's categorical denials, on multiple occasions and under oath, of having any back problem that predated the wreck. I feel my stomach giving way. I am bescrewed. But then, in the nick of time, my survival instinct kicks in. I meet Mildred's blue eyes, my poker face firmly fixed. I hold the file flat above the table for a second, then casually let it fall with a thud.

"So fucking what?"

Her eyes roll backward as she shakes her bouncing hair to and fro. I am wondering if she has caught something from the parking lot attendant.

"Five thousand is it. And that's too damn much. Take it or leave it, it doesn't matter to me."

She picks up the file and exits the conference room in confident stride, leaving me alone to contemplate the looming train wreck this case has become. I don't know whether to laugh or cry. But I must stay focused—maintain my composure. Never let 'em see you sweat. Never admit weakness. Keep a cool and easy manner. I can do it. I've been here before. By God, I'm ready for battle. Bring on Mildred Mahorne and Holston Trucking. But first, I need to talk to Aggie.

$$$

Back in the courtroom, the Honorable J. Cavandar Prickle is engaged with a trio of lawyers, all still deeply engrossed in the same motion hearing that delayed the commencement of Aggie's case. There will be plenty of time to talk settlement with Aggie.

The courtroom is now full of potential jurors. I survey the assemblage, looking for Aggie, while trying to assess the faces of the mass. I am looking for sympathetic, merciful faces—faces of people who can relate to Aggie and her mate, who share their values and their social milieu—the faces of ruffians and road hags. There are a few that look promising. I make a mental note.

Aggie and Billy sit near the back of the room and off to one side. I motion them into the conference room and shut the door behind us.

"They've offered five thousand," I inform them.

"Well, I hope you told 'em they could shove that up their ass," Billy declares.

"I think we ought to consider it. We've got big problems with this case. They've got a file three inches thick full of medical records documenting a long history of Aggie's complaints of back pain. All of it *before* this wreck. Which raises the question: *Why the hell didn't you tell me about all of that and why did you tell them over and over that you'd never had back pain before*?"

"But that's got nothing to do with this," Aggie pleads. "That was my *upper* back. It was my *lower* back that got hurt in the wreck."

"Aggie, that dog won't hunt," I explain.

"But *why*?"

"Never mind why. Just take my word for it. Mildred Mahorne will crucify you on the stand with those records. She'll have the jury thinking you'd lie when the truth would do better."

She begins tearing up. "This is so unfair. I'm the one who went through all the suffering and now they want to call *me* a liar?"

"It ain't right," Billy chimes in. "She ain't the one on trial here."

"The hell she ain't," I correct him. "This all comes down to credibility and we're going to be *stripped naked* of that when the jury sees that medical file." Looking at Aggie, I immediately regret the use of that figure of speech.

"But I can't settle for five thousand dollars," she whines. "My trailer payments are three months behind. I owe my mother money. I still owe my chiropractor. And then there's your fee. I've got to have *at least* ten thousand."

"Tell 'em we'll take ten thousand or they can shove it up their ass," Billy concurs.

It is not uncommon for my clients to evaluate their cases by looking to what they need to net in order to shore up their own financial situations rather than to what their case is actually worth. I have had much experience dealing with such people and I know well how to explain this matter in the simplest of terms. I begin talking to Aggie about the probabilities of the various outcomes. We will probably get some money from the jury, but it could easily be no more than a thousand dollars. The chances for a verdict of over three thousand are less than fifty-fifty. The chance of getting five thousand is remote. And ten thousand is out of the question. I tell her I completely understand that she *needs* ten thousand, but I then go on to painstakingly explain that what she *needs* is irrelevant and must not be considered when evaluating a settlement offer. The object is to get the most money we can possibly get. In this case, all the signs indicate that five thousand is the tops, and if we can get that by settling, we don't need to risk the uncertainty of a jury trial. I lay this all out with lucid, irrefutable logic and wait for her answer. There is a moment of becalmed silence before she replies.

"But I need ten thousand to catch up my trailer payments and pay back Mamma and pay you and—"

"Tell 'em it's ten thousand or shove it up their ass," Billy helpfully volunteers.

We are interrupted by a knock at the door. It is Mildred informing us that the Honorable J. Cavandar Prickle is ready to begin the trial. I rise confidently and motion for Aggie and Billy to follow me into the courtroom. My competitive emotions stir. We are going to trial.

$$$

The first battle in this war will be fought selecting a jury. Judge Prick has randomly assigned forty of the numerous Bedford County citizens summoned for jury duty to serve on our panel. From these, Mildred and I will each strike one name at a time until we are left with the twelve who will decide Aggie's fate. I reconnoiter their faces with uneasiness. Few of the ruffians and road hags I had identified earlier are on this panel. This is not good. Even worse, the panel appears to be disproportionately loaded with bankers, insurance salesmen, and doctors' wives—the worst possible types of jurors for a case like this. I look over at Mildred. There is a smile on her face and a twinkle in her blue eyes.

We begin the *voir dire* of the jury—the process of asking intimate, none-of-your-business type questions of jurors about their personal lives in order to determine what hidden biases they hold that might incline them in our favor. We do this to assure that the jury will be fair and impartial. The term is commonly pronounced *voy dire* in the halls of the Bedford County Courthouse. But Drinkin' Sammy would always correct us, explaining that the term is actually French, not Latin, and that the correct pronunciation is *vowaa dear.* Judge Prick has gone back to pronouncing it as *voy dire* and couldn't care less which is correct. Just another indication of our backsliding since Drinkin' Sammy's demise.

However you choose to pronounce it, *voir dire* is a critical part of the trial because it is the best place to slip before the jury the suggestion that the defendant has insurance coverage that will pay off on any verdict they render. The mention of insurance during the trial is strictly forbidden and will result in mistrials, contempt citations, and other sanctions being visited upon the head of any lawyer who even hints at its existence. During *voir dire,* however, there is some leeway for the skillful lawyer to plant the idea of insurance in the jury's mind. When Drinkin' Sammy was on the bench, there was a lot of leeway: "Now Mr. Juror, have you ever been in a car wreck? And did you have *insurance*? And did the other driver have *insurance*? And who was your *insurance* with? And did your *insurance* pay off on the claim?" And on and on while the other lawyer ranted and raved and objected and raised all manner of hell about "this line of questioning," all to no avail. Drinkin' Sammy would just smile and bang down his gavel and shout, "*Objection overruled*!" Not so, however, with young Judge Prick. One must now be very delicate and subtle with this issue. There is a good deal more artistry involved with the practice of law in Judge Prick's court.

By eleven-thirty, we have selected a jury. We have a doctor's wife, an accountant, and several blue-collar workers, one of whom has been involved in his own nasty dispute with an insurance company. Not the best jury I've ever seen for a plaintiff, but not the worst either. Judge Prick elects to break for lunch once the jury is seated. I decide to dine with Aggie and Billy so that we can review a few last-minute details. As we leave the courthouse, Billy reiterates our negotiating position, just in case it is not clear in my mind by now.

"Tell 'em if they won't pay ten thousand they can shove it up their ass."

I don't even want to know what it is they are supposed to shove.

$$$

The trial proceeds rapidly. It actually comes together much better than I had anticipated. Aggie proves to be a more compelling than expected witness, describing her horrific injuries in a firm and husky baritone. There are even a few well-timed tears as she recounts the months of agony when she hurt too bad to clean houses and fell behind on her trailer payments. Of course, Mildred beats up on her pretty good with the piles of medical records showing the prior back problems, but the damage seems fairly contained. The chiropractor, whom I have paid five hundred dollars for a one-hour appearance, turns in a sterling performance, deftly explaining, with the aid of a rubber replica of the spine, how the impact of the truck caused a "subluxation of the lordatic curve." Things are on a roll for us and I have a good feeling about the outcome. Even Judge Prick, try as he might, can't seem to disrupt the flow of our case. Mildred does not bring up the stiletto heels—she obviously didn't see them. Maybe this will be the break that turns the tide our way.

By four-thirty, we have rested our case and I have delivered a scintillating closing argument. Aggie's fate is now with the jury. Mildred and I reciprocally stroke our egos by congratulating each other on a case well tried. If I am not mistaken, her confidence level has ebbed just a mite. Now the nervous waiting begins. We pace the floors, the halls, the restrooms. Billy races back and forth to the front steps to grab breaths of nicotine. "Relax." My voice cracks under the rush of my own adrenaline. I am ready for this to be over. It is getting nigh time for my evening dose of Jack Daniels.

At seven o'clock, the Honorable J. Cavandar Prickle emerges from his chamber and mounts the bench. The jury has given no sign that a verdict is near. "What in the hell could they be talking about for all this time?" he asks no one in particular.

I decide to venture a wishful guess. "Must still be adding up the damages."

"I don't understand it. This case is as straightforward as you can get. What are ya'll holding out for anyway?"

"Ten thousand dollars, Judge, or they can . . . ." I catch myself just in time.

*"Ten thousand dollars!"* his Honor erupts. "You don't seriously think that jury is going to give you ten thousand dollars for this case do you?"

"We've offered them five, Judge!" Mildred shouts, trying to appear reasonable.

"Well hell, that's reasonable," Judge Prick observes. "You ought to counsel your client to take that and let's bring this foolishness to an end."

I look around to Billy, who is shaking his head no. I can *feel* him thinking where he wants this proposal filed. "We'll wait for the jury," I say.

"Well," thinks his Honor aloud. "We could let the jury go home and come back tomorrow. I'm sure they're all ready for dinner right about now."

"Fine with me, Judge," says Mildred.

"Me too," I say, attempting to be agreeable.

"But then, if we let them stay in there, maybe they'll go ahead and finish up." Judge Prick is going to *starve* a verdict out of them.

"Fine with me, Judge," I agree.

"Me too," says Mildred.

Finally, at eight-fifteen, the bailiff enters the courtroom to inform us that the jury has reached a verdict. There is a benumbing heaviness to the moment and a rush of emotions as the twelve haggard people file into the courtroom.

"Have you reached a verdict,?" Judge Prick thunders.

A demur woman holding a folded piece of paper nods yes. I would never have guessed that she would be the foreperson.

"Pass me the verdict, bailiff," the judge orders. He receives the folded document and fumbles with it for what seems like an eternity. Aggie stands beside me breathing heavily. I can tell she is about to tear up. Finally, Judge Prick unfolds the verdict. He appears to read it over no less than three times. Then his eyes roll backward. Could there be something in the Bedford County water that causes this, I wonder. But then I realize this is probably good news.

"Mr. Bailiff, will you read the verdict?" He hands the paper to the bailiff, shaking his head in bemused disbelief.

"We the jury find for the plaintiff and award damages of fifteen thousand dollars."

"*There* is *a God in heaven!*" screams Aggie.

"*Order in the court*!" Judge Prick bangs his gavel.

Aggie has both arms around me now, squeezing me in a bear hug. Billy is patting me on the back and telling me what a wonderful job I did. I am back in his good graces, at least until his next drunk-driving case. I look over at Mildred, who is gathering up her files as she shakes her head in disbelief, a wry smile on her lips. I am flooded with a feeling of warm satisfaction. Against overwhelming odds, I have successfully waged war for my client. I have battled a tough-as-jagged-glass, grant-no-quarter defense attorney and a tight-ass, plaintiff-hating judge and prevailed, leaving the diffused residue of injustice in my wake. I float out of the courtroom in a sublime state of consciousness. Bring on the next challenge—I am ready for it. I am supremely confident. The meek will surely be dispossessed of the earth if I get the chance to contest the will.

Outside, the streets are calm and the traffic is light. Mildred stands on the curb waiting to cross.

"You did a good job," I console her. "Those are the breaks."

"You too," she begrudgingly allows. "You just can't tell about juries."

"Win some, lose some, I guess."

"I guess."

We cross the street toward the parking deck. It is deserted now, except for my LeSabre and the black Lexus beside it. *Oh shit,* I think as we approach our cars, hoping she won't notice her passenger door.

Down the street, the siren of an ambulance echoes between buildings. I pause to orient myself to its direction. It is coming our way. The flashing red lights produce an eerie strobe effect under the low-hanging ceiling of the parking deck. I glance at Mildred. She stands by her Lexus, door open, ready to enter, but pausing there just a moment to stand, erect and still. We watch the ambulance speed toward us, the excited energy of its flashing lights and wailing siren building with its approach, then peaking as it passes, then ebbing away like the streamers of a fireworks display melting into the night until there is nothing left of it but the echoes within our heads. Our eyes meet for a second, maybe longer, no expressions, no words, just one brief connection between minds that does not seem to require elaboration. She shoots me a coy smile as we turn to get into our cars.

# Nocturnal Birds

To a man at the bottom of life, there is more to look up at—more to see. And less to lose. Small pleasures lie within easy reach, unplundered by other hands reaching constantly upward in quest of grander prizes. At thirty years, Ronnie Arceneaux was looking up at all creation with a storm on his back. In better times, he would not feel the silent thunder rumbling his days or smell the dry lightning infecting his air. And he would not need her to soothe the edges of his discontent or to raise him above his anxious fears. He would not need her to do any of those things for him.

O'Connor's Garage, mid-July. Three bay doors gaped into the scalded afternoon. Outside, lazy platoons of Johnson grass drooped in the swelter, flagged thirstily at sun-blanched fence posts. Pecan trees bowed groundward, pushed by the slow breath of summer. A faded asphalt ribbon meandered toward the horizon like a drunken peddler and a torrid humidity hung in the air thick as gumbo. Birds flew slow, or not at all.

She appeared along the roadside as if the earth had spilled her there, a living piece of the afternoon infused with the terrain through which she passed. Heatwaves seeped from the pavement and bent the distance beyond her and the honeysuckle vines that spanned the barbed-wire fencing waved slow-motion ripples in her wake. Her face was round as a pie, her skin of that rough, tawny hue that confessed of life under an Alabama sun. Rusted-ginger curls spilled in dirty tangles to just below her jaw, roughly assuming the circularity of her face. She was of a bulky, corpulent build, yet there was a gentleness in her manner and movement that was comforting to the eye. A handbag rode her shoulder, suspended by a thick leather strap, and in her hand, a small brown paper sack dangled insignificantly from the end of her stout arm. Her smile was carefree and unworried.

Hulking, redheaded, Claud O'Connor leaned against the bay door's edge, measuring the girl's approach. Across from him stood a ladder, carefully positioned within the threshold, and atop it, a boy wearing a striped work shirt, damp with a day's sweat. In the boy's hand was a power drill and over his chest was patched the inscription, *Biles Overhead Doors*. As the drill whirred, O'Connor looked up at the boy, ramming a toothpick deep between his eyetooth and bicuspid. When the whirring quit, he spoke.

"You gone be through with that damn thing before six o'clock or'm I gone have to stay here with you all night?"

"I'm gonna be done in half an hour, Mr. O'Connor," the boy said, unruffled.

"Not at the rate your slow ass is moving, you ain't."

"Half an hour, Mr. O'Connor."

O'Connor stepped through the door, flipped away his toothpick and spat a brown strand of tobacco juice to the pavement. "I don't mean for you to go rushing through with no half-assed job now. I gotta be able to lock that goddamn thing when we all go home."

"It'll lock for you when I'm done with it."

"I'd hate to have to sue Arnold Biles if somebody come in here tonight and stole me blind because that door wouldn't keep 'em out."

"Ain't nobody coming through this door without a key, wunst it's locked."

O'Connor looked back at the girl, who had just reached the edge of the parking lot. Her hand rose in a friendly wave and he returned the greeting. "Somebody tell Ronnie lunch finally got here!" he shouted toward the back of the garage. Then, looking at the sack she carried, "You might as well just feed him supper now. Late as you are with that."

"The Lord knows I couldn't help it." She sighed. "That Janie Carlisle done gone off to Montgomery again. She done gone off and forgot all about me setting there with her mama. And Miz Merle, weak as she done got, she can't be left alone. So I had to set there waiting on her highness, Miz Janie. Waiting for two hours until she finally come in. And then I got to wait some more, 'cause she got to run me home 'cause I ain't got no car. Then I got to walk here with his lunch. The Lord knows I couldn't help it."

"You need to get Ronnie to get you a car."

"You know he don't make money enough to get me no car, Mr. O'Connor."

O'Connor let go a deep laugh. "He makes a hell of a lot more than what he's worth."

"It ain't enough to get no car with."

O'Connor took a round plug of tobacco from his mouth and hurled it over the parking lot and into the weeds by the roadside. He took a pouch of Red Man from his hip pocket and began cramming the leaves into his mouth. "Miz Merle done hung on for longer than I ever give her."

"Been a slow and cruel cancer," she said. "Sure be a blessing when she passes on."

"You'll have to get you another job then."

"Won't be hard. Somebody's all the time calling me, needing a sitter."

O'Connor turned back to the garage and called out again, raising his voice over the hubbub of clinking tools and idling engines. "Ronnie! Squirrel's here and got something for you."

A tall, solidly built man with thick glasses and a heavy moustache looked up from under an open hood. His face and hands were smeared with streaks of black grease. The glasses stretched his vacant brown irises into a pair of misformed orbs, possessed of neither rhyme nor grace. He caught sight of the girl standing in the doorway and put down the silver socket wrench.

New Iberia, Louisiana, had not been a big enough place for Ronnie Arceneaux to hide. Five years ago he had climbed into the rusted-out pickup with his itinerant great-uncle at the wheel and left his native city in the middle of night, bound for Atlanta. He had just turned twenty-five and he was on the run. The felony assault warrant had been sworn out by the pregnant girl's father, who could not abide the notion that anyone named Arceneaux, let alone one with the mind of a ten-year-old, had fathered him a bastard grandchild. And so Arceneaux had been caught up in a matter of honor, in a world where such matters were settled with fists and tire tools, and when the violence broke out, it was Arceneaux who had quickly seized the upper hand. When the dust had settled and the blood had clotted, the father had little more than the strength necessary to crawl to the nearest telephone and call his friend, the chief deputy with the Iberia Parish Sheriff's Office. Arceneaux knew enough to pack his belongings quickly.

They made it as far as Springdale, Alabama, where the truck and the uncle gave out together. The truck got towed to a junkyard and the uncle taken to the local hospital, where he coughed up a week's worth of blood in two days before making a graceless exit to the next world. Atlanta became no more than a stale plan, two hundred miles to the north and east.

O'Connor soon crossed paths with the luckless stranger and, having immediate need of extra hands and a fondness for a Cajun accent, set him up in the shabbiest of his five shabby rental houses—one within walking distance of the garage. Arceneaux was slow to learn, but the tasks of a mechanic's helper required little insight, and the cost of his muscle, from O'Connor's standpoint, was a square bargain.

Despite his slow-wittedness, Arceneaux proved reliable help and his life soon settled into one of routine and repetition. Although a loner by nature, his persistent daily treks to and from the garage attracted the curiosity of several of the townspeople and he found himself the object of more charity and invitations to Sunday church services than met with his own idea of comfort. He had not the manners or finesse to refuse these random kindnesses and consequently, he became an unwilling, visible fixture to most of the Springdale populace.

The girl he now eyed over the tools and transmission parts and piston rings and scatter of the garage floor had been sent to him six months ago by O'Connor while he was bedridden with an extended case of flu. She was known to most of Springdale's twelve hundred inhabitants only as Squirrel, few of them ever having heard of the name, Mary Garmon. She lived in a singlewide house trailer near Arceneaux and supported her sparse existence with various odd jobs, most of which involved caring for the sick. She had brought him groceries and medicine and even done a little cooking and laundry, and when he got over the flu, she continued to do the same things for him and he did not complain. Nor did he complain when she came to him one evening and slowly peeled away his blue work jumpsuit and then her own clothing, and took him to bed and lay with him until morning, nor even when she brought her toothbrush and the small box of toilet articles to leave for the convenience of regular weekend visits. As he watched her now through the stir of dust off the concrete floor, bringing the small sack that he knew contained a baloney sandwich and a can of sardines, he did not see the thick flesh that hung from her arms or the coarseness in her skin or the chestnut flush of her teeth, but looked instead upon an approaching comfort—a hard-used angel bearing common blessings—and a smile came up under the grime of his face as she waded toward him through the clutter.

"You late wi' dat, ain'cha?"

"Mr. O'Connor says you need to get me a car. So I won't have to count on the mercy of Janie Carlisle to haul me around everwheres."

She handed him the sack and they retired to a corner of the garage and sat at a small wooden table. He unwrapped the sandwich and opened the sardines while she spread napkins over the grimy tabletop. He offered her a sardine, which she took and ate all in one piece.

Morris Cole, the new mechanic, slithered underneath the Ford Taurus parked nearby, his back against a rolling-board. Arceneaux did not like Morris Cole, and he liked being indebted to him even less. He knew Cole had been watching him for weeks and he had felt the menace in his quicksilver eyes and the sense of impending trouble those eyes always drew through his nerves.

It was soon after Cole began working at the garage that the games had started. O'Connor would lock the doors, a wooden bench was turned on its edge, the dice came out, and money went down on the floor. The others showed him how. Sometimes he picked up the piles of cash and sometimes he reached for the money only to have his arm grabbed while another hand swept it away, but he always finished with less than he started. The last time, he had lost it all. They let him sign pieces of paper so he could keep playing, and as the dice kept banging against the bench, he kept signing the papers until O'Connor made him quit. Then Cole would show up every Friday with his friend Thayer, and when the paychecks were handed out, Thayer would cash them for the men at discount, and Cole would be there wanting money from Arceneaux. There had been arguments over how much Cole could have and Cole had made threats, and then he had felt the storm within him that had lain five years dormant. Now as he eyed Cole sliding around under the Taurus, he felt the storm gathering, felt the weight of its building danger, sensed that its next surge would sweep him up within it and there would be nothing he could do and nowhere he could run.

He handed her the last bite of sandwich and took a sardine for himself, and then she cleaned off the table and went up front to wait for closing time, joking with the workers while she waited. She bought them Cokes from a machine and then O'Connor let down the new door and locked it for the night. She put the Cokes in her handbag and they set out together. The sun was low in the sky and the thick air still held the day's heat and the sweat came quickly as they walked. They took the dirt road toward Harley Newman's hayfield and when they reached the familiar cluster of mimosas, they crossed the runoff ditch and he held the barbed wire apart for her to step through and then he followed her into the field. They crossed the field to the pole barn where they were out of sight of the road and sat on the firm ground underneath the shelter of its tin roof, looking west into the setting sun. The field sloped downward before them to a creek, and beyond the creek were woods of oak and hickory with a smattering of poplar and pine, and the star-like leaves of sweetgums were mixed among them all. They drank the Cokes and he threw his empty across the creek and into the woods, and she scolded him for it and put hers back into the handbag. She moved closer to him and began to stroke his back in repeat-ing circles. As the sun worked its way down through the trees, the sounds of dusk rose out of the ground, the crickets and katydids crying to the approaching darkness, then a woodwind of nightbirds, a trio of whippoorwill notes, and he felt the day melting away under the gentle motion of her circling hand. Insect choruses thrummed from the living earth like a heartbeat, and the blood in his veins ran smooth and even, and the storm was far away.

When Friday afternoon came, Thayer was there at the garage door, taking the paychecks and handing out cash. O'Connor stood at the far end of the parking lot, talking with a man from the bank. The banker was writing in a notebook as O'Connor pointed out things about the building. Arceneaux looked at his check. One hundred twenty-two dollars after deductions for rent and taxes. Thayer held out a fifty and two twenties.

"Ain't enough," said Arceneaux.

"The shit you say. A man's entitled to an honest commission, ain't he?"

"You ain't no honest man."

"Now don't you go insulting me, Cajun boy," said Thayer. "If you don't want my services, you can just wait till Monday and take it to the bank."

"Ninety ain't fair. Last time it'a hundred."

"Cost of living's done gone up since last time, Cajun boy. Ain't you ever heard of inflation?" Thayer pulled a five out of his pocket. "Here. Here's ninety-five. Take it now or go to the bank on Monday."

"He ain't got till Monday." Cole's voice was flat—portending urgency. "He owes it tonight."

Arceneaux turned away from Thayer and took a step toward the door. Cole stepped directly into his path. Cole was perhaps a couple of inches shorter than Arceneaux and a good twenty pounds lighter. He had jet-black hair that stopped just before his shoulders and framed the hard-edged features of his lean face. His sleek, muscular build suggested a controlled quickness—as if he could have been a matador in another life. Arceneaux looked at him and felt the boiling inside. He stepped to his right to skirt around Cole, but Cole matched his movement and remained between him and the door.

"Don't you think about leaving here owing me money, you son of a bitch," said Cole.

"I pay you Monday. Monday I go to the bank."

"You gone pay me tonight, you goddamn half-wit. Now sign that check and give it to Thayer and get the money."

"I going home. You get out my way now."

"Oooh! Cajun boy's talking tough now, ain't he?" mocked Thayer.

"Why don't I just go home with you, then?" said Cole. "Get me a little of that stuff you like so much."

"Whacha talking 'bout?"

"Your ugly little Squirrel. I bet that's some good stuff, ain't it Ronnie? Gotta be good for you to hang around with something ugly as that."

"You shut up 'bout her."

"You just take me on home with you and I'll trade out your debt for a little of that pussy. How'd that be?"

"I done said you shut up 'bout her now." He felt the muscles tightening and the swells rising from his stomach and he knew that something wild was loosening inside of him.

"I do believe you done gone and got him pissed off, Morris," said Thayer.

"You pissed off at me, Ronnie?" Cole stepped closer. "Now why would you be pissed off at me? You the one that owes *me* money." He reached forward and put his palm against Arceneaux's chest and gave him a slight push. "You sign that check and give it to Thayer there so's you can pay me. Either that, or you fix me up with a little of that Squirrel pussy you like so good and maybe I'll forget—"

Arceneaux's swing barely grazed Cole's cheek. The force of the punch left Arceneaux reeling off balance and Cole was quick to take advantage. Three rapid blows to the head and Arceneaux was staggering backward, his glasses on the concrete floor. Cole kicked them hard toward the other end of the garage. Arceneaux got his legs back under him and the two men faced off, circling in the garage door, dark blood trickling from a cut above Arceneaux's eye.

The booming anger of O'Connor's voice brought all motion to sudden stillness. He moved swiftly for a man of his size. His hands landed hard against Cole's chest and then Cole was against the wall with his feet six inches above the floor and O'Connor was nose to nose with him. The other men backed away, one went to retrieve Arceneaux's glasses.

"What the hell you think you're doing?" shouted O'Connor.

"I'm just trying to collect my money." His voice quivered. "He swung at me first. Ask any of them."

O'Connor released his grip, but did not back away. "I don't allow that kind of collecting to go on here."

"He's the one swung at me. And he owes me fair and square. You seen him lose it to me."

"How much you figure he owes you?"

"Hundred and fifty. It's an honest debt. I was just trying to collect and the crazy bastard swung at me."

O'Connor pulled a roll of bills from his pocket and peeled off a hundred and a fifty and stuffed them into Cole's shirt pocket. "That oughta make things even. Now get whatever tools you brought in here with you and get your ass away from here. I don't want to see you anywhere around here again, you hear?"

"Fine." Cole's voice broke slightly. He brushed his chest where O'Connor had laid hands on him and paused, as if trying to collect himself. "Just give all my work to your half-wit there and let him finish with it."

"Don't worry yourself about it. We'll get it done without you." Then, turning to Thayer, "And you too. Clear your ass outta here and don't ever let me catch you around here again either."

Thayer's mouth drew into a tight smile that matched his smirking eyes. "And good evening to you too, Mr. O'Connor." He nodded.

Cole threw a few wrenches and sockets into a small red toolbox and climbed into Thayer's pickup. They had not left the parking lot before O'Connor found Arceneaux. He was wiping off his glasses on his shirttail, then holding the scratched lenses up to the light and wiping again.

"You need to be more particular about who you get yourself in debt to."

"Them two ain't honest. They try to cheat."

"Well, now you owe me another hundred and fifty. So there's one more deduction from your paycheck. You gone soon be working for nothing, at the rate you're going."

"I glad he gone. He ain't no count."

"You had no damn business playing dice to begin with. I oughta have put a stop to it. Now I gotta go find me another mechanic."

"It better he gone. He ain't no good. He gone cause bad trouble."

O'Connor pulled a rag from his hip pocket and began dabbing it over the blood on Arceneaux's face. "You better get on home. Squirrel's gone be wondering what happened to you."

Arceneaux adjusted the glasses on his nose and crossed the parking lot. At the road, he stopped and looked back at O'Connor standing in the big doorway with the garage's interior glowing behind him. Their eyes locked for an instant and Arceneaux's mouth opened as if he were about to speak, and then it closed again and he turned back to the road and began to walk.

He took the dirt road and headed for the mimosa trees, and when he reached them, he stepped over the ditch and made his way between the strands of barbed wire and into the field. He found her sitting under the pole barn. The sun was beyond her and low in the sky and the long shadows of the trees stretched out toward her and covered the creek in their shade. She sat silent at his approach and only turned to look at him when he had sat down beside her. Then he felt her hands against his face and she was wiping above his eye with a white handkerchief and when she took it away, there were dark splotches on it. He felt the turning within him and felt the fear of what she had discovered upon the handkerchief and of how he would have to tell her of it. He looked away, but she placed a hand on his cheek and gently turned his face back toward hers. She did not speak, but the questions were there within her eyes and he felt their challenge, and lacking the fortitude for response, he did not make effort to answer, but sat still at her side in the crescendo of dusk and together they listened.

The summer wore on, sultry and unrelenting. Then September came in as hot as July and the men at the garage talked of the heat and the older ones argued over when a south Alabama summer had ever burned hotter. Arceneaux's life fell back into a patterned existence—a routine orbit among things familiar and common. His seas had calmed and the wind blew soft within him, as though spent of its passion, and he felt himself adrift in a welcomed normality.

There came a Friday in late September when the oppressive summer had begun to wane and the advancing dusk encroached steadily, day by day, upon the afternoon. When he left the garage, the west was mottled with bands of blood-orange and sky. As he walked the roadside, a covey of quail burst from the brush before him and took wing in the failing light and he paused to watch their flight. It was full dusk when he reached the dirt road and the half-moon was ringed in mist. Lights from a distant farmhouse shimmered over the breadth of a cotton field and the white bolls caught the light and that of the moon too, and they were as the reflections of stars on a vast and calm lake.

He did not hear the footfalls until he was a hundred yards onto the dirt road and when he first thought he heard them, he turned and saw nothing, so he kept to his path. When he heard them again, he knew he was being followed. He turned and looked into the darkness behind him and saw the shadowy form frozen against the night. He called out to it and there was no answer or movement and he stood looking into the form and feeling the old winds rising inside him and he began to tremble. He took a step toward it and it likewise began moving toward him. Then the familiar voice of Cole came against his ear and the storm within him gained.

"What you got hid out here, Ronnie boy?"

"Whacha want wi' me?"

"I wanna know what you hiding out here. Might wanna get me some of it myself."

"Ain't nothing here for you. You git on." He stood his ground while Cole advanced slowly.

"That ain't a very nice way for you to be talking to me, Ronnie. Not after you done cost me my job."

"I ain't cost you nothing. You jus' ain't no count is why you ain't got no job."

"Listen at you, you half-witted son of a bitch. Telling me I ain't no count. Why you ain't worth the powder it'd take to blow your Cajun ass away and you telling me I ain't no count?"

"Jus' let me 'lone. I don't want no trouble."

"It's too late for that. You done caused me a bait of trouble and now it's fixing to cost you."

Arceneaux saw the vague outline of a club—saw it draw back to strike—and backed away quickly. The blow glanced off his chin and he fell to the ground. He scrambled to a squat and saw Cole coming toward him with the club drawn back and he covered his head with his arms. The blow landed full against his back and he absorbed its force and then rose quickly upward, coming in between Cole's arms. His hands went directly to Cole's throat and locked tightly around his neck. As Cole struggled in vain to free himself, the club fell to the ground. Arceneaux's grip tightened and the fury came whole within him and its strength bore into Cole's throat and the sounds of Cole's breathing became strained as the intake of clogged bellows. His fingers and thumbs pressed harder now and the thumbs found yet a softer spot below the larynx and they dug fiercely downward until no sound came from the constricted throat. The struggle within Cole's body ebbed away under Arceneaux's unrelenting grip, and still he did not release—could not release, because the storm was full within his hands and its savagery was boundless, and the limpness of Cole's body did not ease it, but drove it harder until finally the muscles of his thumbs and fingers gave way to exhaustion and let fall to the ground the lifeless body of Morris Cole.

He stood over the body watching for any movement, his breath labored as an overfired steam engine. He pushed at the body with his boot, and still nothing. "Get up!" he yelled to the ground. The storm was exploding now and its intensity choked him and his breath came in rapid wheezes. He grabbed Cole's shirt at the chest and pulled him to his feet and pled in a faltering voice for Cole to stand, but when he released his hold, the body dissolved into a pile at his feet. Again he raised Cole up and begged him to stand, but this time he felt the wilted emptiness in the flesh he held, and understood the futility of his pleas.

He carried the body a few paces into a fallow field across the road from the cotton and let it fall to the ground among the weeds. Then he walked back to the road and continued down it in his previous direction. His foot kicked against something and he reached down and picked up the club—nothing but a dried hickory branch of a couple inches in diameter. He hurled it with all his strength into the weeds of the untilled field, and the vines and briers swallowed it up and it became nothing more than a part of the earth upon which it had landed. He took deep breaths as he walked, hoping to control the roil that pushed from inside, and he ambled down the road with wasted motion so that time and its passage might soothe the turmoil that coursed within him.

At the mimosas, he settled to the ground, his back against a fence post, and looked into the night sky, distorted from the moisture in his eyes. Then he closed his eyes on the stars and rested his head against the post and filled his lungs with the pure night air. Images of chaos came upon him out of the darkness, visions of terror and pain, fragments of old fears and torments spinning randomly through his head and plundering his thoughts, people asking him questions in tongues he had no ear to hear, moving about him and behind him, their voices familiar echoes from his past but their words dissolving into hostile babble that he could not take into his head, demanding of him what he could not give them or even understand. He buried his face in his hands and felt a cool moisture come over his skin and he sat in that way for a length of time. When he opened his eyes the world he saw was quiet, and the field spread out before him, cold and colorless in the moonlight. The path stretched out ahead, clear and familiar, and he made his way along it through the hay.

When he reached the barn, she was waiting, seated cross-legged with her back to his approach, looking into the woods where the sun had set. Then he heard it, the sound of night bubbling around them, coming to him as a different and unrecognizable song. The rhyme of the crickets and ground-birds struck his ear at strange new angles and the resonance of their calls filtered through him and mingled with his turmoil, and the melding of it all within him was an unstable mixture of solitude and misgiving—a transient and unsustainable mirage that drifted in and out of his consciousness like a windblown cloud. She stood to meet him and when he reached for her, she came to him and drew his mouth to her own. They embraced, one against the other, both at home inside the night and among creatures who shun the daylight, who assume earth's colors and burrow into their secret wombs to wake with the fall of darkness and fill the night with their song. The half-moon dripped its milky light over them and they stood together in the fragile richness of their moment, a universe from the world beyond their darkness. He traced the contours of her face with his callused fingers and they waited there, the two of them, the world turning toward them, bringing the future toward them, bringing its threadbare bounties and used-up hopes, bringing all that it had left to give them.

## Aftermath

There is a quality in the act of waiting that the mind will not accept—a peculiar sort of cruelty to be endured while life flows by in extended seconds and interminable minutes. The preciousness of time can only be appreciated by looking backward into it—in regarding the past from the perspective of the present—and there is nothing in a moment of waiting to suggest that time is anything but a tormenting enemy or that the sluggish evaporation of the present into the future speaks of a thing worthy of cherishing.

These things I know: the intensive care waiting room of St. Margaret's Hospital, the arrangement of the furnishings, the endless argyle patterns of the carpet, the scratches on the laminated tabletops, the picture of Mary, the infant nestled at her bosom, how the frame hangs slightly askew of plumb, the path to the women's restroom, the magazines scattered about the end tables, pleasant faces smiling up from their covers. I splash cold water over my wrinkled face and return to talk with my waiting compatriots. The second hand of the wall clock twists painfully through its orbit as we ponder aloud the concerns of the moment: the cafeteria food, the Lord's grace, measurements of rainfall. And we wait for threads of news—word of a spouse or a parent. Or of a seventeen-year-old daughter.

The doctor visits daily, but I must be quick. He is busy . . . important and burdened with many patients. His answers are brisk and always the same. They leave me wringing his words like a sponge for some droplet of hope. *The bullet entered through the forehead, didn't exit the skull. If it had she wouldn't still be with us. Her vital signs are stable. Too early to know the extent of the damage all patients react differently to these injuries we just have to wait.*

Barton comes with fresh slacks and a blouse. Another four-hour interlude and we are allowed through the steel doors and around the nurse's station. Fifteen minutes and counting. We hover above her and Barton brushes against me. I inhale his salty odor, feel his burlap hand seeking out my own.

She lies entwined in a mesh of tubes and wires and flickering, hopeless machines, her head shaven bald and swollen to an alien bulk. We stand soundless, our words stuck to our hopes, watching. The nurse will soon remind us that our minutes are spent.

Hopes are fragile. They wear away like sandcastles before a hungry tide. Barton's strength is with the tractor and plow, with the banker, with the cotton brokers. There is nothing more he can do here. Or nothing less. I walk him to the lobby and listen to his pleas. I should come home. For just a few hours, for rest, for a bath. I hold him and feel his weakness—that fear at the bottom of his emotions. He fights to conceal it but I have known him too long. He receives my smile and leaves.

At 2 a.m. the rules are not so hard. An extra five minutes is precious. I lean on the bedrail and hold the near lifeless hand, remembering each year in the curvature of her fingers: the way these hands once held things of value, her grandmother's porcelain figurines, or a fishing rod, dark eyes against the float, the fall of black hair over her shoulders. Have they held a lover too? Have they caressed the moist, naked muscles of a back, or raked through tousled hair under a scalding summer moon? I remember how that sudden quickness would wind through her—that youthful thrill of risk, the love of danger so reckless in a boy but contained within her. I take this room's sterile air into my lungs and my eyes are closed, though I do not remember shutting them, and I hold on against the rail and the memories

The nurse's hand tightens against my forearm. There is a stirring, delicate but real—a definite and sweet movement. The heavy lids quiver. Once, then again, unsuccessful, but an attempt. Tiny spasms bubble in her face and suddenly her eyes are open and the large brown irises burst into the cutting overhead light. Immediately they disappear and the nurse hurries to the wall switch. As I stare down into the dim fluorescent glow, the eyes reopen. I look into those eyes, my two hands wrapping her one, and beneath them is an empty, haunting space that I tow to harbor against the leeward side of my heart. I steady myself, connecting to the hand's bony framework and willing my own strength to meld with hers. Then the eyes slide toward me and hold me for too brief a moment before the thick lids fall back and she lies motionless in the weak light. I anchor myself against her hand and order all reference around it, and when I am certain that the wispy resistance within it was real—was the distant echo of conscious intent—I release the hand and carefully place it over her chest.

The memory of that vast hollowness beneath the eyes overfills me, probabilities and potentials stalking me as I return to the waiting room to consider tomorrow. A new door opens, but a fear that my mind cannot surround has followed me through it, carried along in the memory of those eyes. I think of the future, no longer sure which way to direct my hope. I am ashamed of such indecision and angered by my own selfishness. The weight within me shifts, presses me from different angles, some sharper, some smoother. But I have passed through this door and I will remain here until the next one opens. I am braced for endurance by the movement of her head and the lifting of her eyelids and the shimmer of brown irises swimming in a bottomless ocean, and the bracing is good, like the numbing roundness of strong whisky.

## The Girl at the Fountain

Bradley Biblow featured himself an excellent judge of character—a man capable of quantifying that particular human attribute just as a team of accountants might tongue the tips of sharpened pencils and calculate the net profits of a business venture. And not just Character, but a practiced evaluator of Capacity and Collateral as well. The three C's they called it in the sterile and starched-shirt world of money-lending. Bradley Biblow knew that world from the inside out. Not that *he*, mind you, was ever going to lend anyone any of *his* money or, for that matter, any of somebody else's money. No sir, that was not the kind of thing for Bradley Biblow to do. But it was a fact that others *did* do that sort of thing and when that sort of thing was done, the sterile and starched-shirt world of moneylending in general and the Farmers and Merchants Bank of Montgomery, Alabama, in particular demanded that someone should overlook the shoulders of the moneylenders to see that they had done their job with circumspection. And so enter Bradley Biblow, loan auditor at the Farmers and Merchants, who spent his mornings, noons and afternoons at a small oak-veneer desk, scaling mountains of manila folders that were the debts of the farmers and ginners and cattlemen and timber barons and land developers of south-central Alabama. A stack here for the ones that were solid credit, a stack there for the questionable, and yonder, stacks for the doubtful and hopeless, all neatly classified, if not with pure Aristotelian logic, then at least with methodical Biblowainian analysis according to the profession's accepted criteria—Character, Capacity, and Collateral.

Biblow's fourth floor office window framed an appealing view that looked directly east up Dexter Avenue toward the old State Capitol building. Whenever he needed a respite from the concentrations of his job, he would lift his eyes up Dexter to the exact spot under the front portico of the Capitol—a spot marked with a bronze star—where Jefferson Davis had stood to take the oath of office for the presidency of the Confederacy on February 18, 1861, some one hundred and three years ago. Then he would leisurely wander his mind down the width of the avenue, by the state office buildings and bustling shops that lined either side, to the ornate Italianate fountain which spread across the plaza at the bottom of the street, like some great sprawling birdbath come there to settle, that the pigeons and mockingbirds might frolic in its gushing turrets and spires. Biblow coveted his window with a nervous apprehension that he might at any time be dispossessed of it by some jealous superior, and indeed, it could certainly be argued that even though the office was tiny in size, the location and view it afforded was much above what might be considered commensurate for a thirty-three-year-old loan auditor with a mere four years' tenure. But Bradley Biblow had come into possession of his office fairly and squarely and serendipitously, and he thought it most unjust that someone else might be able to wrest it from him by so simple and unfair a ploy as pulling rank. So as he sorted through his files, he fretted away many hours in angst over the prospect of losing his prized location, even though no one had ever so much as suggested that they would like to have his office or that he might have to move to make room for a more vital employee of the Farmers and Merchants.

One beautiful April morning as a placid breeze alive with the sweetness of pollen dust and birdsinging stirred the papers on his desk, a pensive Bradley Biblow stood at his window, easing his way down Dexter. When his eyes reached the plaza, they fixed upon a curtain of flowing black hair that spilled down the back of a young girl seated on the fountain's stone base. Some of the faces milling about the plaza were familiar to him, but he had never seen this girl before. She wore a white blouse and a dark-colored, full-length skirt decorated in floral patterns and cut from a lightweight fabric that the wind sculpted into ripples. She looked out through thin-gauge wire-rimmed glasses to a paperback that she held in one hand while resting the other against the fountain's base. Her profile held Biblow's gaze and he studied the delicate structure of her face as she absorbed herself in the book. He felt a comforting softness in her appearance—a suggestion of innocence and purity that he found pleasing to contemplate.

As he watched her delicately turn a page, his musings were interrupted by the familiar footsteps of Nash, the loan officer, in the hallway outside his office. He turned anxiously toward the door as Nash entered without a knock.

"Mawnin Biblow," he growled in a gravelly baritone. "Fine mawnin it is too, huh?"

"Yes sir. It is a fine day, sir," said Biblow, scrambling into his desk chair.

Nash's bull-like heft pressed tightly against his smooth white shirt. His sleeves were rolled to the elbows and his tie loosed. His wide forehead glistened with a mist of perspiration even in the cool spring air and above his forehead, thin locks of oily hair spread carefully across a bald spot of crown and appeared to stick there as if pasted. He held an unlit cigar between his fingers and he brought it to his mouth as he settled into a straightback chair across from Biblow.

"Damn fine day, son. Damn fine un it is."

"Couldn't agree with you more, sir."

Nash shuffled his large frame about in the chair and propped an ankle over a knee. He twirled the cigar over his tongue and then removed it from his mouth.

"I'll get right to the point with ya, Biblow. I'm here about that LeMaster Chevrolet account."

"Got that file right here," Biblow said, picking up a thick folder and carelessly spilling a sheaf of papers from it.

"Aw shit, Biblow. I don't need to see the damn file. I jes wanna talk to ya about the loans. Make sure you unda*stand* all you need to know about that last refinance I did for 'em."

"Well . . . aahhh . . . you know Mr. Nash, there are some things that . . . well . . . you know . . . some *irregularities* . . . that I noticed in going through the file. Now nothing, I think, that can't be fixed, you know, but . . . ."

"Now hold on there, Biblow," Nash growled as Biblow fumbled through the spilled papers like a hapless schoolboy searching for a lost homework assignment. "Now there ain't *nothing* wrong with this loan that you need to go worrying about. Aw, there might be some little nit-shit *technical* slip-ups in the paperwork. But that loan's solid as the Rock 'a Ages. I been lending money to Jason LeMaster for twenty years and . . . and goddammit," he banged his fist against the desk, jarring Biblow, "his credit's as solid as any at the bank."

Biblow looked sheepishly away from the red glow of Nash's face and toward the window. He couldn't see the fountain from his desk, but he imagined the girl sitting there, book in hand and in deep contemplation of secrets he longed to share. He cleared his throat as he turned back to Nash.

"I'm sure everything will be all right, Mr. Nash, but I . . . uhhh . . . don't really know . . . is this really proper? Mr. Cravits . . . if he knew you were talking to me about this—"

"Biblow," Nash said softly, motioning him forward with a crooked finger. "Lemme tell ya something about Cravits. Cravits is a . . . ." He leaned in and cupped his hand to whisper, "A . . . *communist*. That's right, Biblow, a *communist*."

"Oh, Mr. Nash. I really don't think—"

"Now I know what I'm talkin about, Biblow," said Nash, rising from his chair. "You listen to what I tell ya. You listen to me and I'll look after ya. And don't go saying nothing to Cravits about any nit-shit technicalities with that loan, you hear? You listen to me and I'll take care of ya." He opened the door and turned back to Biblow for a parting shot. "Nothing to Cravits about this now. Remember what I told ya about him."

Bradley Biblow watched the door close and then he listened to the footfalls of Nash fade away down the hall. When they were gone, he rose and walked back to the window. The girl had vanished and a couple of plump gray pigeons had taken up residence where she had sat. He raised his eyes to the Capitol portico and began afresh the descent of the gentle slope of Dexter Avenue. He freed his mind to flow among the milling pedestrians and he allowed the slow tug of gravity to pull him downward toward the fountain and to the frolicking birds that played within its waters.

* * *

Biblow lived with his mother in a modest old Victorian house just a short walk south of downtown—a once stylish area of the city now caught in the undertow of urban decay. His father, who had been a salesman for the Capital Typewriter Company, had died unexpectedly three years ago leaving her a little more than an arm's reach away from her former circumstances. But she and her only child Bradley managed to get along, keeping the bills paid and the old house maintained to something approaching an acceptable appearance.

"That Myrtice Beam," fussed Mrs. Biblow as she brought a deep dish of squash casserole to the table. "Can you imagine? Bringing that colored couple to church like that. Saints and archangels, what's this world a-coming to?"

Bradley's eyes were focused on the silver tea service resting on the sideboard. He was replaying the morning's conversation with Nash in his head. He wished he had been more assertive with Nash about the deficiencies in the loan documents. Frustrated, he sat reconstructing the conversation over and over in his thoughts, each time firmly explaining to Nash that he would have to bring the matter to Cravits's attention and that Nash had better not be suggesting that he do otherwise.

"Not that I've got anything against the colored folks," Mrs. Biblow continued, her words flying over Bradley like a gaggle of newly-freed doves. "But they've got their own churches, don't they? Why do they need . . . here Bradley, have some squash. And take some of these green beans too. You don't get enough greens and you're sure looking a mite pale from it."

"I just don't know about Nash," Bradley said to no one in particular. "I'm going to have to set things straight with him." He spooned some of the vegetables onto his plate. The black house cat slipped stealthily into the dining room and inched its way along the far wall.

"That Myrtice Beam," Mrs. Biblow continued, reaching

for a sprig of freshly cut mint and dropping it into Bradley's iced tea. "Why *would* she want to ask them to *our* church? Take more of those beans, Bradley . . . . If you ask me, it's just to make trouble."

"Yes, I'm going to have to talk with Mr. Nash about this," said Bradley. "He's interfering in my work and I'm not going to have it."

"I think you're working too hard, Bradley. Up at that bank all day long and cooped up in that little pen of an office. It's not healthy. Why, it's positively . . . *Magic!*" she shouted abruptly, turning at the cat who had suddenly taken to pawing at some invisible disturbance in the oriental carpet.

"I'll see him first thing tomorrow. I'll talk to Cravits too, if need be." His voice now trumpeted confidence.

"I just don't know what Myrtice Beam is *thinking*. The idea of it . . . . Bradley, will you *please* eat your beans?"

That evening, Bradley Biblow, as was his custom, retired to his bedroom at ten o'clock sharp. As he slept, he dreamed of the girl at the fountain. He dreamed that they were standing together by a sparkling lake. They threw bits of bread into the water and there were ducks that swam toward them and ate the bread as it floated on the surface in the girl's reflection, and he dreamed that he was happy and he felt the waves of the lake moving within him like the rushing of blood and the movement soothed him as he rested so that when he woke, he felt refreshed and the girl's reflection came strong among his thoughts.

* * *

The next morning and every morning following for the next week, a forlorn Bradley Biblow stood at his office window scouring the plaza about the fountain with a hopeful eye. Up and down Dexter he went, but she was nowhere to be found. Slowly, he resigned himself to the reality that she had been no more than a passerthrough—the object of a destiny diverging from his own but for that one brief temporal intersection when he watched her among the fluttering birds and cascading waters. He tried to put her out of his thoughts and focus instead on the problems with Nash and the LeMaster loan, which he had done nothing about despite his nightly resolutions to address the matter. He knew that Cravits would soon be asking for his audit report on the file, and he debated with himself about how big an issue to make of the defects for which he knew Nash would be held accountable.

It was two weeks later when he spotted her again. He was lowering his window in order to lock it for the evening. Her posture and position, the small details of her appearance and movement, were all as before and he stood lost in his thoughts, admiring her in the brightness of the slow spring afternoon. He tried to make out the title of the book she held, but the distance was too great to allow his eyes such a trespass. He watched her for several minutes—until he began to feel silly and self-conscious standing there alone, as he was. Then he took the elevator to the ground floor and set out on a path home that would take him across the plaza. She was there, turning a page of her book as he passed. He slowed his pace, thinking perhaps to stop, maybe even speak, but he could not think of what he would say, so he walked on.

She appeared there every day for the next week, so he made a daily ritual of this walk across the plaza, each time yearning to speak to her but never finding the words. Once, she looked up as he passed and for a fleeting moment, their eyes brushed. Bradley's chest surged and he quickly looked away, afraid that his face might betray what churned within him.

It was purely by chance that they finally spoke. It was a Saturday afternoon, Bradley was standing with his mother at the grocery checkout. Suddenly remembering the empty bottle of milk of magnesia in the medicine cabinet, he turned back to remind her that it needed replenishing. And there she was, studying the tabloid rack, her fine coal-dust hair tumbling almost to her waist. He looked away, stunned at seeing her, and then he looked back again. She turned and they were suddenly face to face. She smiled and uttered a soft "Hello," which he returned. That was all. That was enough. Bradley floated out of the store, oblivious to the constant chatter of his mother's voice as they made their way to the parked car and then on toward home.

The next Monday as he left his office, he saw her again at the fountain. They exchanged greetings, and he ventured a comment on the beauty of the afternoon. She nodded and smiled in agreement. He passed close enough to steal a glimpse of the book she was reading: Thoreau's *Walden*. He thought the Lee Street Bookcellar would still be open so he circled the block, doubling back out of her view. Finding the shop abuzz with customers, he entered and purchased his own copy of *Walden*.

He crossed the plaza each afternoon, passed a bit closer to her each time and each day spoke a few more words, much in the way that a wild bird picking up the scatterings from a human hand will, day by day, inch closer to the source of its bounty. He began reading *Walden* each night before bed, staying up long past his regular hour, and he found in the book ideas and thoughts that he had reflected upon before in the depths of his own private existence, and he thought how strange and wonderful it was that someone had thought to write them down in so clear a way and to make a book of them.

That Friday's overcast sky held the promise of rain and a cool, storm-charged wind blew from the hilltop and down the avenue toward the plaza. People scurried from shop to shop along Dexter's broad sidewalks, carrying raincoats and unopened umbrellas and looking apprehensively over their shoulders at the gathering thunderheads above the capitol. Leaving his office, Bradley approached the girl with a fresh self-assurance and the courage to broach a subject beyond the weather. She responded, and soon he was seated next to her on the fountain's base and they were talking of their jobs and their backgrounds. Her name was LaStella Marconi. She worked in a boutique a block off Dexter, a small dress shop owned by her second cousin. Her home was Boston and she'd come to Montgomery to experience southern culture and work with civil rights organizers. As they talked, Bradley studied her unmade face with the scrutiny of an auditor, measuring the length of her delicate eyelashes, the width of her narrow brows and the fragile curvature of her china-doll cheekbones. He marveled at the strange smell of her perfume, her soft New England accent, and the way her earrings dangled against her skin. The first raindrops had dotted their reflection in the fountain's surfacewater before he ever felt the wetness against him. He looked at the sky, holding his palm upward, then he looked back at her and she was smiling and the rain was beading across her glasses.

They got up and she took his hand and told him to follow. Across Dexter and toward the river, toward the warehouses, then up a small alley with narrow sidewalks and weather-hewn brick walls and the rain coming harder upon them, then around a corner and through a screen door and they were standing in a dimly-lit room full of tables and chairs and the air was brimming with a medley of cooking and spices and stormwhipped air. She led him to a table and they sat while a large black man brought them water and a wrinkled cardboard menu in handwritten ink.

The man called her Stell and asked her how she'd been and handed her a hand towel, which she used to dry her face and glasses before passing it to Bradley. Chairs skidded over splintered hardwood with a grating sound and he noticed, as his eyes adjusted to the light, that the room was stirring with people. Looking around, he saw that the patrons were all black and that he and LaStella were the only white people in the room and he felt a nervous shudder pass over him that he tried to conceal. Then he felt her hand against his arm and their eyes met and he relaxed in the comfort of her smile. They ordered supper, chicken for him, a vegetable plate for her, and they drank iced tea from large Mason jars. She introduced him to the waiter—a man named Henry Fellman who also owned the café—and he reached tentatively for the meaty black hand and shook it firmly once he felt the other's grip.

They finished their meals and got up to leave, stopping at a small counter by the door where he paid the check. The rain had quit and the streets were shrouded in thin vapors and the dusk smelled of a spent rainstorm. He walked the quiet streets with her to the bus stop on Madison. A church bell pealed six times as they waited. When her bus came, he helped her on board and then stood and watched it as it climbed and crested the hill. His mother, he knew, would have supper waiting when he got home and would want to know where he'd been. "Had to work late," he rehearsed in his head. "Busy, busy time at the bank now," he would tell her. "Feeling a little spent too. Not really up to supper tonight." Then he would retire to his room and continue with his reading of *Walden*.

* * *

"These all appear in good order, Bradley," Cravits proclaimed with his usual immaculate enunciation, his eyes studying the last file of the stack through silver half-moon glasses. His expansive mahogany desk was cluttered with all manner of calendars, pictures, paperweights, and whatnots. Behind him, the massive oil portrait of C. Malone Townsend, the bank's founder, stared down at Bradley from within a baroque gold frame whose swirls and curlicues meandered happily about in marked contrast to the drab, melancholy tones of the painting. The portrait was hung so that the steely gleam in C. Malone Townsend's eyes was focused directly upon whoever happened to occupy the chair where Bradley now sat—a circumstance very much apparent to Bradley as he waited for what he knew would come next. "*But* . . . ." said Cravits predictably.

"But what, sir?"

"I notice on my list here that you've had that LeMaster Chevrolet file in your office for some time now. Are there any problems there?"

"Oh, no sir. Just haven't gotten to it yet, sir. I'll get right on it."

"Promptness in these matters is essential, Bradley. We are a team here, each of us a cog in a larger machine and with our own job to do. If any of us neglect our work, even for a day, this bank cannot function with the smooth efficiency that our customers have a right to expect. Do I make myself clear, Bradley?"

"Very clear, sir. And I'll get right on it."

"Have it on my desk by tomorrow then. That is all."

The flood of light outside the dark-paneled office brought a squint to his eyes. The adrenaline swelled through him. He knew that the problems with the LeMaster loan were much more serious than what Nash had represented and that his audit of the file would mean real trouble for Nash. And given the hierarchy and office politics of the bank, what meant trouble for Nash was bound to mean trouble for Bradley Biblow. Back in his office, he gnawed at his fingernails as he considered the dilemma. He decided he had no choice but to make his report to Cravits and let the chips fall where they would. But it was nearly lunchtime, so he decided to postpone the work on the audit until the afternoon. He walked to the open window hoping to catch a glimpse of LaStella, but she was nowhere to be seen, and so he let his thoughts wander where they would and soon he was thinking of *Walden*, and she was there in his mind with him and they were watching ducks swim toward them as the sunrays pirouetted on the wavecrests and flashed diamond sparkles up to their faces.

* * *

The next morning, Bradley turned in the audit to Cravits and waited in daily angst for the expected fallout. Each afternoon, he met LaStella at the fountain and the trials of his job quickly melted in the softness of her voice over the bubble and spray of the waters. They talked long into the evenings about things he had never discussed with anyone—of man's place in nature, of breaking with the conventions of society, of race relations, civil disobedience, and so much more. He mainly listened at first, asking questions now and then, trying to make sense of this whole new way of looking at the world that was opening before him.

He took the car that he shared with his mother and took her to a Saturday matinee at the Capri. It was a love story about an American expatriate in prewar France. It ended in the tragedy of Nazi occupation. She told him that the movie was about searching for an internal freedom in a world where choices are imposed by codes, customs, and taboos that suck the free will from humanity and that ultimately breed its destruction.

"But how can we survive without our customs and laws?" he asked her. "Doesn't that lead to chaos?"

"Do you consider yourself an enlightened man?" she asked him. "A man intelligent enough to choose how to provide for your own needs without having those choices imposed upon you?"

"Of course," he answered.

"And you do not see it as chaotic for *you* to pursue *your* own needs as you see fit and without being told how you must go about it?"

"No, but—"

"But other people are told every day what they must do, how they must live, how they may and may not go about providing for the necessities of life. Some are told in words having the force of law, but others are enslaved more subtly. By social conventions that rob them of their independence without them even realizing it. And these, Bradley, are the most enslaved of all."

"And am I one of those people? One who has lost his freedom without knowing it?"

"Ah, Bradley," she said, putting her hand gently on his shoulder. "That is for you and you alone to sort out."

They drove to her apartment, an upstairs, one bedroom affair in a substantial old brick quadraplex on the east side of town. She got them apple juice and set a bowl of grapes on the coffee table, and they sat on her couch and she talked to him of her beliefs about vegetarianism and how she abhorred the idea of eating animal flesh. He asked how her bones could stay solid without eating meat and she laughed, shaking her head, and her long hair fell across her smile and down over her breasts and Bradley could not help but to reach up to brush it away. She gently touched his hand and he took hers and their eyes were each within the other's and then he felt a perplexing new energy humming within him and he let himself fall toward her closing eyes until their lips met. They held each other there in the long sunlight of the afternoon and then she was leading him to her bedroom and there was a ceiling fan turning slowly overhead as she slipped her skirt to the floor in one prolonged flow of motion and then pulled up her blouse and released her firm bare breasts to the muted bedroom light. He took her in his arms, their naked bodies touching at a thousand points, and then he felt her heat, felt her smooth, flat stomach against his own and the deep glow of her eyes washing over him, and the smell of perfume on her skin was strong in his head. They sank to the bedsheets and floated there upon them and she was like nothing he'd ever imagined and he felt himself above her and within her and their breathing came in heavy unison as they struggled in shared ecstasy under the slow-turning fan until they could stand it no longer and their cries came together in the explosion of their release.

There are many ways for an existence susceptible of consumption to be devoured. After that Saturday afternoon, Bradley became the willing captive to a pleasure he had never known. LaStella was his shepherdess. He came to her whenever he could withdraw from his other world and they made fevered love in the dragging, fan-twisted air of her bedroom and they drank from each other's passions like children with unquenchable thirsts.

She introduced him into her circle of friends where the tabooed and forbidden were the norm. There was Henry Fellman and six or eight others, blacks and whites alike, and they dressed in clothing that was unusual to his eye and they talked in a new way and of different ideas that he did not fully understand. He sat with them on the long Sunday afternoons at LaStella's apartment and they spoke openly about themselves and about love and freedom and sometimes he felt as though he had stepped through a looking glass into a world where up was down and what had once been right and natural was now in a state of crumbling decay. She played records while they visited, a music foreign to his ear with disharmonic chords and with melodies that climbed haplessly toward a resolution they never seemed to reach. Sometimes Henry would bring records for her to play and the raw sounds of the guitar and the gravel-throated voices of the singers would rasp against his overmatched ear like an angry locomotive. Some brought handrolled cigarettes of an acrid, burned-rope odor to pass among the group and when he inhaled the smoke he felt the vibrations of the floor and walls around him and the music came to him in strange new ways that gave him a pleasurable understanding of its disharmonies and unresolved melodies.

At work, he found it increasingly difficult to focus and the pressures of the matter with Nash churned inside him. Then word came of Nash's resignation, under pressure, it was rumored, and afterwards when he talked with the other loan officers, they seemed guarded and distrustful of him. It occurred to Bradley that the loan officer's position would probably be filled from within the bank and he gave fleeting thought to seeking the position himself, even to the point of making discreet inquiries to his supervisor about the matter, but the supervisor wasn't encouraging and his ambition to pursue the advancement soon dwindled.

As spring gave way to summer and summer to fall, his relationship with his mother became strained and contentious and he found himself continually lying to her concerning his whereabouts. He felt guilty about the lies and considered moving out and finding his own place. Many days he would sit at his desk, scanning the yellow pages of the telephone book for realtors, but whenever he would start to place a call, something would distract him and off he would go in another direction and the call was never made.

It was an early October afternoon when LaStella came to see him at the bank. It was the first time she'd visited his office and when he saw her, his heart jumped and he knew that something was amiss.

"Henry's been arrested," she told him between rapid breaths. "We've got to bail him out."

"Arrested for what?" he asked.

"Why does it matter *for what*? Arrested for being Henry. For speaking his mind. For standing up for a principle. We've got to help him."

He'd never been to the city jail before and the smells of human confinement and bad cooking and antiseptic concrete and steel overwhelmed him and he felt waves of nausea spilling over him. A uniformed woman led them through hallways filled with officious bustling to a police captain who sat behind a desk looking at them with the eyes of a leopard stalking its prey. He asked them a lot of questions and then tossed a form down on the desk and showed Bradley where to sign. They waited in steel-back chairs in the stale-aired hall until Henry was finally brought out. He had bruises about his face and his eye was swollen shut. They took him home and helped clean him up and when they were sure that he was all right, they left. He watched the tears drip slowly down her cheek as he drove her back to her apartment.

That evening they sat in the swing on her screened porch and looked out through the trees over the dimly lit street. The night was cool and quiet, except for an occasional passing car. He could not see the features of her face in the dim light, but he knew there was a distance in it that he had not known before and he felt a despair falling gently through him.

"Is there anywhere that a person can go and find real freedom anymore?" she said to the night as much as to him.

"But we're free here. How much more freedom do you need?"

"You were brought up to think that you are free. But look at you, Bradley. Consider your life. Free to go into your bank at eight o'clock sharp each morning? Free to wear that stiff white shirt, that tie? Free to go home to your mother every night and put yourself at her whim and disposal? You're not free, Bradley. Why, you're less free than Henry, who can't even eat in a white man's restaurant. Who can't even drink out of the same water fountain. Can't even piss in the same pot as you because of the bigoted fears of the fools who make the laws you order your life around. Henry is a freer man than you. His life is constricted by an outside world that doesn't have the sense or compassion to shed its tyrannical customs. But you, Bradley, are the warden of your own prison. One that you have built around yourself and that you don't even see. Your life is a clockwork of order. You are trapped within it and you have not the slightest idea of how to escape. You read the words of Thoreau, but you do not hear his voice—it does not sing in your heart."

He looked at her, she looked at the floor. The swing

creaked. In the distance, an ambulance's siren. He could feel her tears in his heart.

"I don't know what you mean. Do you want to run away? To live in the wilderness?"

"Not the wilderness."

"Then where?"

"Boston."

He felt a lump rise within him as the weight of her words settled.

"This is not my home, Bradley. I can't continue living here. I never intended to stay this long."

"When . . . when will you . . . ."

"I don't know . . . . Soon . . . . I'm not sure."

He walked to the screen and leaned against the framing. It occurred to him that he'd never considered how this all might end. He wanted first to ask her to stay and then he wanted to ask if he could go with her and then he didn't know what he wanted or how to give words to his jumbled emotions, and so he stood looking into the vague form of the sycamore tree that shaded the porch and on through its branches into the night beyond.

He stayed the night with her and clung passionately to her and when the empty dawn broke, he left her there sleeping. He phoned her time and again from work that day, but there was no answer. In the evening, he drove by her apartment and stopped on the street in front, but no lights were burning and he didn't get out. For two days he tried in vain to reach her and on the third, he drove to the apartment again and banged against the door until a neighbor came out and told him she had moved the day before. He went to the restaurant and found Henry moving among the tables in his stained apron. "Left yesterday. Going back to Boston," he said, wiping off a tabletop with a wet towel.

"Did she leave an address? A telephone number? Anything?"

"Not with me. No way I know of to contact her."

There were the two weeks of accrued vacation time, and Cravits was more than happy for him to take them. "You just haven't seemed yourself lately, Bradley," he said. "I think a short time away from the bank will be just what the doctor ordered."

He spent the time in an aimless whirlwind of urgent energy. He tracked down the members of her circle. None had heard from her or knew how to contact her. He regularly drove by her apartment, desperately hoping that she might return for some forgotten item, but she didn't come and soon a new tenant had moved in.

The two weeks leave expended, he returned to the bank and slowly fell back into that ordered world that had once been enough to fulfill the whole of his existence. But now, a newborn hunger smoldered within him and it continued unsatisfied and he felt the vacuum it left around him. He made a practice of eating lunch a couple of times a week at Fellman's, and he came to enjoy being the only white patron in the restaurant. He would occasionally ask his co-workers at the bank to go with him, knowing that the invitation would bring rejections and nourish furtive whispers about his strange new behavior.

When he resolved to find a place of his own, he broke the news to his mother in a firm and unyielding voice and her tears no longer held the power over him that they once had and he considered how this was like a freedom of sorts, and it reminded him of LaStella and their last conversation. A small rental house on the south side of town would be just the thing for him, he decided, and so he contacted a realtor and began checking the classifieds. He looked at a couple, but neither struck him as what he wanted and so he continued looking.

That December, a notice appeared on the office bulletin board announcing that the vacant loan officer position would be filled, and Bradley resolved to place himself in contention for the vacancy. This time, he went directly to Cravits with his intentions, but again, got little encouragement. Still, he persisted, polishing his résumé and filing the formal application. He found a challenge in the process that filled some of his emptiness and he relished the new tension it brought to his life.

It was early January when Cravits appeared at the door of Bradley's office—the first such visit with which he'd ever been honored. His spirits rose at the sound of Cravits's well-manicured voice. "Bradley, I wanted to speak with you personally about the loan officer position. The interest you've shown in this job, as well as your diligent work here at the bank, have not gone unnoticed by the management." His heart began to thump. "Unfortunately, we have decided . . . ."

He didn't hear the other words about the successful applicant's superior qualifications or about how he was close, but not yet quite ready, for such an important position, or about how he should be sure to apply again when the next position became available. He didn't see Cravits leave his office or see him look back with his sympathetic, condescending smile. His eyes were fixed on the opposite wall and his only thoughts were of how he would, once again, walk the several blocks to the old house and, once again, spend the evening listening to his mother's voice. He got up from his desk and walked to the window, closed now to keep out the winter. The sky was gunmetal gray and the atmosphere pregnant with gloom. Unfamiliar faces milled over the plaza. They walked past the fountain without so much as a glance toward it—as if it were nothing more than an impediment intersecting their most direct route between origin and destination.

He returned to his desk and sat. A newspaper was spread across it, open to the classifieds. As he picked it up, his eyes fell upon the "Ticket" heading. He instinctively read the first entry: "FOR SALE: Plane ticket. Montgomery to Boston. One way. $20 or best offer. Call 272-8461." He looked at the window, then back to the paper. Then he read it again. He picked up the paper and folded it and held it in one hand and tapped it against the top his desk. He got up and walked back to the window and looked out at the fountain. A small boy stood at its base and behind him, an elderly woman. The boy tossed a coin into the water and turned and smiled at the woman. She handed him another coin and he tossed it into the water. The wistful outline of a smile crept across Bradley's face as he turned away and walked to his desk. He opened the paper and read the ad again. Still there, same as before and staring right at him. He put the paper on the desk and studied the number. Then he picked up the telephone and began to dial.

## 29 Years, 7 Months, and 18 Days

*REPORT*

TO: Potomac Mills Headquarters in Baltimore, Maryland.

FROM: Billy Redmond, Bogatachee River Mill, Teasdale, Alabama.

SUBJECT: Burney John Scaggins (commonly knowed as Coot).

FACTS: On Tuesday, August 10, Mr. Burney John Scaggins, white male, age about 45, asked General Manager Dalton Staffordly if he couldn't have off Wednesday, August 11 and Thursday, August 12, due to he had personal family business to tend to. General Manager Staffordly declined due to he had done been out too much in the last two months. I was witness to this. On Wednesday, August 11, Mr. Burney John Scaggins was not at work. On Thursday, August 12, Mr. Burney John Scaggins was not at work. On Friday, August 13, Mr. Burney John Scaggins come back to work. Mr. Burney John Scaggins stated to General Manager Staffordly that he was out on Wednesday, August 11 and Thursday, August 12, due to he had went to Mobile on a family matter. These are what I know as the facts, being what I seen and heard with my own eyes and ears.

* * *

So that was my report to headquarters. Keep it simple. Stick to basics. You don't get paid for thinking. Don't get no raise for having opinions. They asked for the facts, you give 'em the facts. Now don't get me wrong—I liked old Coot. But all that's beside the point. Business is business when there's a mill got to be run. We all got jobs and responsibilities. Mine's to be secondhand in the first-shift spinning room. Others got their own problems. They wanted me to tell 'em what I knowed. Officially tell 'em—the bigwigs up in Baltimore. Like any of 'em up there gives a shit. But it ain't for me to question why. Ask me for a report on the facts, you gonna get just that. You do what you're told. Keep it simple. You don't get paid for thinking.

But I won't soon forget that day it all went down. Early August and hot enough to draw your sweat in the shade. Staffordly had got to work before seven that morning—got there just as I come up—and had his secretary, prim little Ms. Shankle, sashaying along two steps behind. Now this itself showed me there was some kind of mischief about because the big office don't usually open up till eight which is a whole hour after the first shift starts. And when I seen Coot come walking up toward the main door five minutes after the seven o'clock whistle had blowed, I knowed right then and there that the flywheel had done been set to spinning and the shit was fixing to be throwed to it. Just walking right up like nothing was wrong, wearing that same dirty tee-shirt he'd wear like it was the only stitch of a shirt he owned, already sweaty and pulled down not quite all the way over his squat belly and him scratching at hisself with them stubby little fingers like some dumpy looking troll that had done crawled up out of a Dixie Dumpster. No siree, you didn't want to get downwind of *him,* not when he come in in the morning and for sure not when the three o'clock blowed. And him coming in five minutes late like nothing had happened after what he'd done already to piss Staffordly off? Not that five minutes was gonna make a damn bit of difference about what Staffordly was gonna do. It just seemed that this oughta been one morning for sure that Coot got to work by seven. Hell, he oughta got here by a quarter of and been standing at his warper, ready to doff off the first beam soon as the night-shift boy quit.

But Coot never seen things like other folks. Not when he started working here after he'd got old enough to legally drop out of Teasdale Junior High School—he never made it to high school being he flunked several grades—and not in all the days and years he come to the spinning room, usually before the whistle blowed and almost never late, and stayed hard at it for eight hours a day, five and six days a week. Didn't never get sick and didn't hardly ever miss a day, except that time he had the hernia operation. True it was, he worked like a port-city whore, worked at his same damn warper, doffing the big beams and half the time not even going out on break with the others, not stopping much to talk or joke around—Coot wasn't never much of one for a joke anyway—but he just never did have what it taken to get nowhere besides his one machine, which was where they kept him ever since he started here. Maggie Zigler used to tell him—she was always kidding him, always kidding with everybody—that Potomac Mills was gonna put up a gold plaque with his name on it right there on that warper. Gonna say, *Put here in honor of Coot Scaggins, master doffer*. She'd say that to him and rub her hands up and down that old thick, dirty arm of his real slow-like and twitch up her eyebrows and smile at him like a pie's coming outta the oven. Then she'd walk off in them tight jeans she'd wear and that denim wrapped around her thighs close and smooth as watermelon-rind. The men, they'd all fix their eyes against them jeans till she got down to the end of the spinning frame, where she'd always turn back and wave and smile and all of 'em would wave and smile back and some would even whistle. Except of course for Tony Woolenbarger who never, to my knowings, showed no interest in no woman. And except for Coot. He'd just stand there with that half-open mouth looking in no particular direction out through them Coca-Cola bottle glasses with eyes big as navel oranges. Not smiling, not frowning, but just looking around like he knowed he was at the center of some kind of mischief though he didn't know what, but looking like he was enjoying it just the same. And now here he come walking up from the parking lot five minutes late and Staffordly already in his office pissed as hell and waiting for him like a goddamn repo man come to get the family car.

Just about the time Coot hit the main doors, Ms. Shankle come prancing outta the big office and started off down the front hall. She come heading in my direction to where she and Coot was gonna run dead-up on one another before he could get out in the plant and get to his machine. I kinda slipped back out into the plant myself since being second in charge of the spinning room I had things to see about on the floor there. But I stood so as to keep my eye on what was gonna happen out in the hall with Coot walking straight toward the spinning room and Ms. Shankle coming in on him at nine o'clock and neither of 'em knowing what kind of surprise they was headed for. And sure enough, she run right up on him where the halls come together and poor Coot no more than fifteen feet from getting to the spinning room door. Next thing, she was in his face and he's just standing there with that mouth half open and them big empty-looking eyes. Then she's fussing at him like some old-lady schoolteacher fixing to rap some mischief-maker's knuckles, them little glasses hanging from her neck just a bouncing against them skinny tits, and ol' Coot's reaching up with that meaty hand and scratching that dirty looking three days' or so worth of growth across his face that was always there and was always causing the rest of us to wonder about how he kept it so, 'cause he never shaved it off clean but it didn't never seem to get no longer neither. I couldn't hear nothing that was being said over the slamming and fussing of the machines, but you didn't have to hear nothing to know she was giving him holy what for, standing there eye to eye with him, her face red as November sumac, and him with that froze-up look just sliding backwards just the least little bit with them big eyes straight on her, and her moving right with him to stay right in his face whatever he done. Then she sorta grabbed him by the shoulder and pointed down toward the big office where Staffordly would be waiting and off they went down the hall, her leading the way and Coot following two steps behind like sin after the devil.

Being the second hand in the spinning room for the

last four years, I knowed I'd be wanted in Staffordly's office sooner or later. I already knowed about the whole mess anyway 'cause I'd gone up with Coot when he'd asked to have the last two days off to go to his brother's funeral in Mobile and seen how Staffordly had done laid the law down about it, saying that Coot had done missed too many days when he'd been out with his hernia operation and that he couldn't run no cotton mill if it wasn't never going to be nobody there to work in it. So we left Staffordly's office and I told Coot I was sorry about his brother and that I was sorry he'd have to work and miss the funeral and all but that I'd done what I could about it, telling Staffordly we could get by a couple of days without Coot if we just had to. And Coot, as was his way, didn't have nothing much to say about it, but his face let you know he was real hurt. So I figured that sooner or later Staffordly would send for me to come down while he done whatever it was he had in mind to do to Coot, because Staffordly was just the kind of person who needed to feel like he had somebody there backing him up whenever he done something that was gonna cause waves.

And while I'm shuffling around the spinning room waiting to be summonsed, here come that damn Tony Woolenbarger to see what was going on, because he'd done caught a glimpse of Ms. Shankle out in the hall spitting brimstone all over Coot and since he knowed about Coot's situation with the funeral and all, he'd done halfway figured out what kind of trouble was brewing. Now you talk about a different breed of cat, here one was. Not from nowhere around Teasdale, I'm proud to say. Come in here from St. Louis a few years ago and why—don't ask me. He was tall and rail thin and wore his hair to below his shoulders and pulled back in a ponytail like a gal, except you'd never mistake him for a gal because he was ugly enough to gag a maggot. Had a face full of big, deep wrinkles that was always broke out with what looked like pomegranate seeds. Lived alone—well, he did have a cat that he was always talking about that had one eye and two names—and drove a dingy yellow Volkswagen van that he'd take anywhere. Took it down to New Orleans once to see one of them rock groups—the Grateful Dead I believe he said it was. We all heard enough stories about that trip to make us appreciate Mississippi for being between us and there. Going down there with his damn one-eyed cat, Sid Arthur he called it, and prowling through the French Quarter. "Trucking through New Orleans with the Dead," he'd say. "Tripping out in Louis Armstrong Park. Man, it was so cool," he'd say. He seemed to kinda take to Coot, as much as anybody could take to Coot, and got right pissed off at Staffordly about him not letting Coot go to the funeral. Had a lot to say about it to the men on the floor, about Coot being exploited by the company and about Staffordly being a stooge for the bigwigs up in Baltimore and on and on about that sorta thing. Course he never said none of it to Staffordly's face—at least not at first. Well, Woolenbarger sees Ms. Shankle out there wagging her prissy finger in Coot's face and comes to me to find out what's going on. Now it ain't my job to pacify him or keep him informed about mill business and besides, I didn't know myself what was going to happen for sure, though I did have a pretty fair feel for the situation. So I told him to get his longhaired ass back to his machine and not worry hisself about this business and that I'd let him know something as soon as I knowed myself. He didn't like it none, but what could he say? He already knowed as much as me about the situation anyway, and there wasn't nothing to do but wait and see how high Staffordly's stack was gonna blow.

Well sure enough, it wasn't hardly two minutes after Ms. Shankle had gone off with Coot that she come right back to the spinning room to get me to come down to the big office. When we got there, Ms. Shankle politely showed me into Staffordly's office where he set behind his desk leaning way back in his chair underneath an eight-point buck hanging on the wall behind him—not really a very nice-looking mount I didn't think, something uneven and screwy-looking about the rack. He always seemed to me to look the same every time I seen him, with his wiry little frame in that same old light blue short sleeved shirt—maybe he just had a closet full of 'em, all the same color—with that damn plastic pocket protector with *Potomac Mills* printed on it, full of more ballpoint pens than a banker's desk, and the same ugly red, white, and blue tie.

Coot was setting in a plain wood chair across the desk with both feet flat on the floor and them callused hands resting like cantaloupes on his knees. I'd been in Staffordly's office a million times and it always had that smell of cotton lent just as strong as out in the plant. And in the summer, you'd think that his window air conditioner that run all the time would sorta take some of that smell out of the air. But no, it was always as strong as if you just went right to the middle of the plant and breathed in deep. Just smelled a lot cooler was the only difference. And there Coot was, looking up at me behind them thick glasses with them dark black eyes and that look he'd get with his mouth half-open and chin hanging down and you feeling like he just don't really know for sure what the hell's going on.

"Come on in and shut the door," said Staffordly.

"Yes sir," I said and took a seat next to Coot.

"All right, Skaddens, do you want to tell me where you were the last two days?" Staffordly asked.

Coot couldn't look him directly in the eye. "Went to mah brother's funeral. It uz in Mobile."

"Well hell, Coot, I thought we'd talked about you going to that funeral." Then he looked at me and asked, "Didn't we talk about Coot going to that funeral? I sure do believe we talked about that very thing and as I recall we decided we couldn't spare any more man-hours for such as that. Am I remembering right, Redmond?"

"That's what I remember you saying," I said.

"Well, Coot, do you remember something different?"

"Mista, he uz my onliest kin. I ain't got no other. No other brother ner sister ner wife ner noboby. I jus hadta go mista."

"But we discussed this Coot. Don't you remember that we discussed it?"

"I ain't got nobody else, mista. I hadta go."

"You had to go? Well I had cloth that I needed to get made. That's why I'm here. To see that cloth gets made. I'm not here to run a funeral parlor. And I remember we had a clear understanding that you would be at work and not in Montgomery or Mobile or wherever your funeral was. Hell,

Coot, you've already missed a whole bunch of time with your surgery and all. A man can't be taking off from here whenever he wants for any reason he comes up with."

"Mista, I been at this here mill fer twenty-nine years, seven months an eighteen days. I been here eva bit o'that time mista and I worked hard eva day I uz here. Twenty-nine years, seven months, an' eighteen days."

Now I thought that to be pretty good counting for a man that don't even read not even a newspaper, and I looked over at Staffordly thinking that's probably just about right, but he just set there leaning back in that chair looking at poor Coot like a judge about to pass sentence and the quiet of that moment just hanging in the room while Staffordly played with the end of his tie. Then he leaned forward kinda sudden and looked at Coot like he was gonna try to stare a hole right through him.

"Coot, I'm sorry, but I got to have people working here who can follow directions and come in to work when I tell them. I can't have folks working here who come to work whenever they want to and lay out whenever they feel the need."

"But it uz mah brother's funeral." His voice commenced to rattle like he'd ate a loaf of toast and ain't quite swallowed all the crumbs. "You gotta understand, mista. He uz all the kin I had. He uz all. And all I done wuz go fer his funeral. I done worked here twenty-nine years, seven months, an' eighteen days mista. Twenty-nine years, seven months, an' eighteen days."

Now Staffordly looked over in my direction like he was waiting for me to come in with something, but I just set there and held my tongue 'cause he plainly had the situation well in hand and it really wasn't nothing for me to say. After all, he had done told Coot not to miss them two days of work. And I guess you can't keep a cotton mill running if you can't tell who's gonna be coming in to work from one day to the next. So after what seemed like a while, I guess Staffordly figured out that I didn't have nothing to add and so he went on with Coot.

"Were you here in this office Tuesday and did you hear me tell you that you couldn't have off to go to that funeral?"

"I heered ya, mista. I heered ya, but he uz mah only brother. I hadta go, mista. I hadta go."

"I got no choice but to let you go, Coot. I got to know when my hands are coming to work. I can't have people laying out when I tell them to be here."

"But I done worked here twenty-nine years mista. Twenty-nine years, seven months, an' eighteen days."

"You're fired, Skaddens. You can come in next Friday and pick up your last check, or you can tell Ms. Shankle and she'll mail it to you."

"Twenty-nine years, seven months—"

"That's it, Coot. Go on home." Staffordly rose up from under the buck's head. "That's it. Now go on home so everybody else can get back to work."

I walked back down the front hall with Coot and told him how sorry I was and watched him walk back through the big doors and out into the parking lot for the last time. It was one of them kind of things where your insides is telling you there's something not right even though on the face of it, he had done disobeyed a direct order of the general manager. But life's gotta go on, as it's said, except that ain't the way Woolenbarger seen it. He was waiting at the door when I got back to the spinning room. I went ahead and told him what happened—wasn't no need to keep it a secret now—and he just turned and walked off mad as hell, not saying nothing. Just kept to hisself the rest of the day, brooding over his machine, then went home at three o'clock without speaking to nobody.

It was over the weekend that a big storm blowed in off the Gulf. Come in on Saturday night and I mean it rained to outdo Noah's flood. It was still raining Monday morning when I left for the mill, and the streets and roads was covered with water. Hit a low spot on South River Road, flooded out my pickup and made me late for work. When I got there, Woolenbarger was huddled up with several of the men—Maggie Zigler was there too—and they was all looking over a piece of paper Woolenbarger had. They didn't pay me much attention, just kept on with what they was doing for a minute or so and then went back to their machines before I had to say anything to 'em. Then later that morning I found out about that piece of paper. Norris Tatum, an ugly little critter well knowed to have a mouth big as a lawyer's ego, come up to me at break to fill me in on it. Seems it was a petition Woolenbarger was getting up about what happened with Coot and it had a lot of choice things to say about Staffordly. Tatum says to me that Woolenbarger's going around getting all the people he can to sign it and gonna send it up to Baltimore to the main office. Well I knowed that if Norris Tatum knowed about Woolenbarger's petition, it wouldn't be long before Staffordly found out. And sure enough, I was right. It was just before noon and Staffordly and Ms. Shankle was headed out for lunch when they run right up on Woolenbarger, who was making his way from the men's room back out to the floor. Staffordly starts right in on him.

"Where's your petition, Tony?" he says.

"Ain't for your eyes," says Woolenbarger.

Then Staffordly says, "We'll see about that," and goes to reaching for Woolenbarger's back pocket, where there's a folded up piece of paper.

"Get ya damn hands off me," says Woolenbarger and pushes Staffordly back, and all the time Ms. Shankle's looking on real shocked like—like somebody's done pulled down their pants and showed her something she ain't never seen before, except in pictures. Well, Staffordly kept coming for that paper and Woolenbarger kept pushing him off, and then he called Staffordly a worthless little turd and with that, the two of 'em wrapped up together like a Lance's super-thin pretzel. They went at it all down the main hall, scraping and scuffling, neither of 'em landing much of a punch, until they was at the main doors going to the parking lot.

Then Woolenbarger, showing more strength than I ever figured he had, gets his hands somehow up under Staffordly's armpits and lifts him right off the ground and right through the doors and out into the rain they go with Ms. Shankle running after 'em hollering "Stop it! Stop it!" as loud as she can go in her flimsy little voice, and me and several of the men following to see what was gonna happen. Now right outside, there's this graded area where they leveled off the parking lot and it's fairly steep and at the bottom of the grade is a drainage ditch. And wet as it was, water was coming down through that ditch like the Bogahatchee River itself. Well, Woolenbarger carries Staffordly right to the edge of the grade and I don't know if you'd say he shoved him or throwed him but he hit that grade and commenced to rolling downhill like a screeching sack of potatoes. There wasn't nothing for him to grab to and no way for him to stop until he hit the water. Luckily, it wasn't no more than knee-deep at the bottom. Me and Josh Bingham went crawling down to help pull him out, but by the time we got to the bottom, he'd done got to his feet and was standing there wet and muddy as a giant pollywog, and that red, white, and blue tie all wrapped around his neck like a striped eel. Next thing, we heard this belly-splitting laugh from up above and I didn't have to look to know it was coming from Woolenbarger. And when Staffordly heard that, he didn't need no more help getting out of that ditch. He started clawing and scraping his way up that bank, falling back now and again and getting muddier and muddier, but he kept on coming, and I never heard so many *goddamns* and *sons-a-bitches* come outta one mouth in such a short time in my life. And judging from the look on Ms. Shankle's face, I'd say neither had she.

Well, when Staffordly got to the top of the bank, he was fit for strangling puppies. Trouble for him was Woolenbarger was nowhere to be found. He'd done got in that yellow Volkswagen van and took off like Mario Andretti, but I swear I could still hear that sucker laughing like a Mad Hatter. And if I had to guess, I'd say the rest of 'em was hearing it too, except maybe for Ms. Shankle.

Of course we never heard from Woolenbarger again. He musta followed through with sending his petition to Baltimore though, because it wasn't long after that I got called into Staffordly's office to meet with one of the bigwigs. He set there in the same chair where ol' Coot had set when Staffordly canned him, all bull-necked and bald-headed, wearing a dark suit and looking serious as Jesus at the Last Supper. Staffordly leaned back in his chair under his squirrelly looking buck and asked me to tell the bigwig what happened with Coot and then with Woolenbarger, and so I told what I knowed. Then the bigwig asked me to give him a report in writing about "the events leading to the termination of Burney John Scaggins's employment with Potomac Mills," so I done that too. Now it's well knowed that won't nothing ever come of all this and I'm sure as truth that my report's just been filed away in some drawer, probably next to Woolenbarger's petition. But I guess it gives 'em a little something different to worry with up in Baltimore besides making cloth. Everybody gets in a rut now and again and if flying down from Baltimore to Birmingham and then driving from there to Teasdale will get some bigwig out of his boredom, then why do I care? Just be nice to 'em: "Glad to have you here, sir. Come back again and visit our mill anytime, sir."

I seen Coot about a week ago. He'd taken a job pumping gas at Red Malone's filling station. Didn't look like the same Coot to me. Said he was having trouble with his stomach where they done the hernia operation. Said it bothered him so much he was thinking about applying for disability. I wished him luck and that was about it. That's about as deep as any conversation with Coot ever got. I guess everybody's got their strong points and weak ones and deep conversation ain't one of Coot's strong ones. You'd have to say, being honest, that Coot never had many strong points to him. It makes it all the more strange, him remembering things like how many days he worked for Potomac. Sometimes, I try to work out how long I been with 'em and I can barely come up with how many years I been down there, let alone the months and days. But I can tell you that Coot worked for 'em for twenty-nine years, seven months, and eighteen days, and I reckon that's one of them things I won't never forget, even though knowing such a fact is about as useless to me as tits to a boar hog. But I guess it was important to Coot to keep up with such as that. And he done good at keeping up with it too. Like I say, we all got our strong points.

## A Christian Burial

Now look upon this. A stout water oak, craggy bark carved by time and weather, foliage half-stripped by a bleak winter, the clefts of its branches nested with mistletoe. See the girth of its trunk, how it has ridden the back of time and spread itself year by year into this sublime form. Feel the chill of this baleful wind and the emptiness of this season, the amorphous emptiness of this place and season.

But imagine now a summer, a river of afternoon light cascading over this trunk, and shadows too, as the earth wheels about just so. Sharp and distinct shadows, maybe a passing human form, maybe the silhouette of a child. Maybe a child at play.

Now behind you, yonder. The rising church steeple. Beneath it, whitewashed boards and steep-pitched rafters and weeping window glass, all fitted together by long-forgotten hands, the hands of farmers and moonshiners and horse traders, the hands of people who settled this high-ground before collective memory can recount, folk of common desires and simple hungers. They built their dwellings upon the rise of this hill that they called Mt. Shiloh, maintained (and still do) themselves and their kin under the shadow of this church, the Mount Shiloh Pentecostal Church, in a place where life runs slow and family names endure through the generations. Read them in the inscriptions on the mailboxes—the Sorrells, the Pickwoods, the Jarrells—in the engravings of the wet-gray headstones, the same names. They endure as the church and its lustrous steeple with the cross there atop it, the cross set upon its pinnacle, positioned at just the proper angle. Watch it catch the slant of summer's blazing sun. Imagine that summer, the dense and sweltering heat, the sun moving slow along its orbit, the shadows circling the churchyard, circling over the ground as if searching for something lost.

Now watch the cross. See how it creeps through the northeast churchyard, through the cemetery that spreads across the sloping ground. See how it works its way resolutely through the headstones, then beyond the cemetery and toward the water oak. Watch as it approaches the great tree. Watch and imagine.

Understand that this is just a game. A child's game. Something spun from innocent imaginations. An idle engagement for passing the time when a slow summer extends the daylight and bakes copper clay ground into parched and sorrowful earth and tawny dust stirs high under a whirlwind of bare feet and jump ropes and footballs and dragging, sultry breezes. Imaging them as the game begins. They will watch out of corners of sharp eyes as the cross slinks over the ground, will watch in their cautious play until it joins with the water oak's trunk. And when the full shadow of the cross is cast against it, the play and the noise and the laughter will cease with a stunning suddenness. They will stand as bronzed statues, maybe a leg lifted here or an arm extended there, while the shadow marks its spot on the tree. For one minute, then two, time will arrest itself and all motion will freeze except for the slight but inexorable movement of the shadow across the breadth of the tree trunk. Then the horizontal bar of the shadowy cross will complete its path and fall once again upon the ground, and then the noises of running feet and child-laughter will rise again from the churchyard.

To new and uninitiated players, a rare thing in this remote part of Georgia, the game will be explained with vibrant eyes and the exhilarating conviction that only children know. When the shadow is full against the tree, Satan is loose on the world and searching for souls. The cross, fixed as it is above the ground, affords no protection from the evil that suddenly threatens. The only salvation is to stand quietly in place, lest you be detected, and wait upon the return of the cross—for some fragment of its shadow to brush the ground and redeem the earth from this lurking danger. The slightest sound, the smallest movement, and the souls of all could be lost. It is a game played on lazy, sweltering summer afternoons by the children who inhabit this highground on the outskirts of Hobsonville, Georgia—this ground called Mt. Shiloh. Remember that it is only a game.

* * *

Ephrum Jarrell appeared silently out of the murky dimness, his hulking form and man-odor filling the doorway between the hall and front parlor. Gray, angry brows arched over intense eyes that gave a steely reflection, even in the pale and failing light. Thinning white locks crisscrossed his head, a few falling randomly down into his age-spotted face. The muted lamplight glowed amber against the opposite wall, bathed the end of the gray metal coffin in soft, dying tones before fading into an arc of blackness. The woman turned to him, seated in her corner, but he looked past her, past all that the room contained. The silence held. Only their slow breathing stirred the air. From the hallway behind him, the case-clock's pendulum throbbed a steady beat.

Finally he spoke, his voice heavy with age, the words coming sandy and rough. "How long's he been here?"

And then her voice, soft as the lamplight but steady—no hint of falter. "They brought him about an hour ago."

"When's Laura getting in?"

"Plane gets to Atlanta around ten. Be after midnight before they get here."

"Who's picking 'em up?"

"Gonna rent a car."

"What about Jacob? Where's he?"

"Out."

"Out where?"

"Out."

Then a settling—stillborn quiet retaking the room. Hands in pockets, he crossed the floor, stood, eyes downward, plundering the young shut-eyed face. Her gaze followed him—remained fixed as if some revelation were about to escape him.

"They done a good job for him. I was afraid maybe . . . ."

His voice trailed off—the thought retracted.

"He looks at peace. Can't ask for no more than that . . . him being at peace."

"What about the funeral?"

"Wanna do it day after tomorrow. In the afternoon. Can you arrange with the deacons?"

He paused, looking down into the pale, becalmed cheeks. "I'll see about it."

"I'd be appreciative."

After a moment, he backed away. "I won't wait for Laura and Adam. I'll see 'em tomorrow."

"Just come . . . whenever."

"In the morning then."

He turned to leave, paused at the door. "You shouldn't wait in here. You oughta wait out in the kitchen. Not in here."

"I'm okay. I'll leave in a minute."

He stepped through the door and stopped again, looked back through the edges of his eyes. "I'm sorry, Elizabeth. It's a hard thing, this is."

"It's a hard thing, Ephrum."

"We make our own choices in this life."

"We do."

"Martin made his. Made some wrong ones . . . took a wrong path. We make 'em and then have to live with 'em. And others has to live with the loss."

"You know it too, Ephrum . . . what it's like. What it's like to lose a son."

"I do."

"And now a grandson."

"Now a grandson."

"I don't wanna hear about bad choices, Ephrum. Not now. Don't wanna hear about any wrong paths. Not even about God's law and who's broke it and who ain't."

"God's law don't change for not talking about it, Liz. Breaking it comes at a high price."

"Don't wanna talk that now, Ephrum."

He turned away into the hall—paused there inside the sepulchral beat of the case-clock. "You're a good woman, Liz," he said. "I'm sorry about Martin. Truly sorry."

Then he was gone, his boots echoing through the hall, to the front porch and fading, then on the wooden steps and fading still, fading into the empty solitude of the moonless night.

* * *

Adam Knight tried to focus as he sipped his morning coffee, elbows propped unmannerly on the kitchen table. Too many scotches on the flight down, too little sleep in a strange bed. His thoughts were as scattered as dandelion fluff, and this would be a day when thoughts would need to be well-harnessed.

Laura had been up an hour—already dressed, walking in the yard with Liz, mother and daughter consoling, grieving. The call had come yesterday afternoon while they were dressing for a benefit, a black-tie affair, lawyers mostly, like him. He'd been looking down on the East River, straining to see through the light mist that shrouded the city in thin, muted colors. From behind him, he had heard her emotions bursting, the frantic timber in her voice. Then one side of the conversation, the words "pistol" and "by his own hand" explaining it all with a stab. A wave of resignation had broken over him as he absorbed her voice and gazed into the despair of her youthful face, a face of ten years' less wear than his own. Then guilt, as he selfishly considered the pending disruption of his life, the appointments and conferences that would need to be rescheduled, deadlines that would need extending. They would, without question, fly out that evening.

He sipped the coffee from a mug wrapped loosely between his hands, looking out over the rim at his approaching brother-in-law.

"Sleep well, Adam?" Jacob Jarrell asked as he reached for the coffeepot.

"No complaints, Jake."

"Where's Mom and Laura?"

"Walking in the yard."

"Guess they've got some talking to do, huh?" He settled into a chair opposite Adam.

"No doubt." Adam considered the uncanny resemblance between Jake and his late brother. Both had round, soft faces—skin fair and smooth as wax fruit. The look of their father. And nothing at all like the grandfather, neither in physical appearance nor demeanor. Papa Ephrum's seed lay dormant in this branch of the family tree. A good thing too, he thought.

"So what about you, Jake? What are you up to these days?"

"Me and Sam Stillman's opened us a garage. Rented an old filling station in Hobsonville and opened it up."

"How's business?"

"Not bad for just getting started. Got enough work to bust up our knuckles on."

"But not good enough to get your own place, huh?"

"Not yet. But that time's coming."

Adam looked around at the empty kitchen, came back to Jake. "What the hell *happened* with Martin?"

Jake's eyes fell on the table. "It just finally got to be too much to take, I reckon. Him with his . . . you know . . . you know what he was."

"A homosexual."

"He liked the . . . the men, you know."

"And the word got out?"

"Got to be knowed of. Too many knowed of it. It ain't something to tell. I mean . . . Martin was my brother. It didn't matter with me. But it ain't something to talk about. Maybe in New York it's all right to tell. But not around here."

"Who did he tell?"

"Just a few at first. Then anybody. Everybody. He just went crazy over it. Told me he was sick of it . . . of keeping it secret and all. That there wasn't nothing wrong with him and he was gonna quit acting like there was. I tried to tell him it was crazy. People may know anyway, but they don't wanna hear it. Even them that knowed expected him not to talk about it, to make out like he was normal. I guess that's what he got tired of. Playing like he was something he wasn't."

"Shit." Adam sighed into his coffee mug. "How did Liz take it?"

"For a few days she'd bust out crying whenever you tried

to talk to her. Then she got better about it. It was Papa Ephrum that was trouble. I knowed when he started talking about it that Papa Ephrum was gonna be hard on him. Talking about him being an abomination, about turning from Jesus and all that. It was real hard on him . . . real hard."

"How's your mother doing?"

"Mama's a strong woman—"

Jake stopped speaking as the back door opened and his mother and sister entered the kitchen. Adam turned in his chair to face them. Liz Jarrell's smile was as demure as her stature—soft as the rounded edges of her face or the large brown irises that looked out gently from under her thinning brows. Her dark-henna hair was pulled back with a barrette, exposing a triangle of olive forehead. She moved toward Adam with a natural, pastoral grace, walked into his open arm without speaking and put her own around him.

"You ladies have been out early," he said.

"We had a good walk, huh Mom?" said Laura. "A good walk and some good remembering."

"Yes we did, dear. Bless y'all for being here. It means . . . ." She paused to collect her emotions. "It means a lot to me."

"I'm sorry, Liz," said Adam. "It's hard to find words at a time like this."

She nodded, then gently pushed Adam back into his chair and began to massage his shoulders. "I guess you boys are ready for some breakfast," she said. "What kind of a host am I . . . you sitting here with nothing but coffee."

"Don't worry about breakfast," said Adam. "I don't eat it anyway. Jake and I can get something together for you two."

"Jake cooking breakfast?" said Liz, shaking her head, a smile forced against her lips. "Now that'd be something to see."

They were clearing away the breakfast dishes when Ephrum Jarrell entered the front door without a knock. He came directly into the kitchen, greeted Adam and Laura, small talk about their flight down. His speech was guarded and laden with a ponderous tenor that hinted of a weight carried within him that was about to be dropped. He asked if he might speak with Liz in private. Adam and Jake rose to leave, but Laura objected, insisted they all hear what it was he had to discuss. The old man resisted but Laura's resolve was unwavering. When it became clear that his granddaughter would not relent, he finally yielded. They sat at the kitchen table, Papa Ephrum at the head. He looked at the salt shaker in the table's center as he spoke.

"The Board of Deacons met this morning. At the church. There's a lot of concern about this funeral. A lot of . . . objection to it happening at the church." He paused as if to measure the reaction to this as it settled over the table—then resumed in the same voice. "Martin died in sin. Done to himself something only God had the right to do. Lived in sin too. Lay man with man in unnatural union. Some of the deacons . . . they don't want no church-funeral. There's even objections to him being buried in the church cemetery. There's a lot of concern . . ." His voice trailed off into a painful, pulsating silence. He raised his eyes, looked around the table, met the four pairs all focused back against him, met them one at a time, no one flinching, not a lid batting. And no question among them as to where the hush had settled or whose silence it was to break. She let it lie on the air, gave it time to wrap its portentous unease around them. The softness in her eyes vanished, transformed into hard walnut irises that seized control of the silence, eyes that carried the quiet fire of her self-assuredness. She fixed them upon the disheveled asymmetry of Ephrum Jarrell's face, ran them along its craggy ridges and down its age-carved canyons with feminine relentlessness. When she finally spoke, her voice rang with a resolve woven within well-contained emotions.

"What are you saying, Ephrum? Come on out with it."

"These things are decided by vote. You know that. There was a vote taken."

"And what did you say to them, Ephrum? How did you vote?"

"What could I say? It's all there in black and white. He lived in sin . . . died in sin. I can't change that. Nothing . . . nothing can ever change—"

"Our family *owns* a plot in that cemetery. Martin's daddy—*your own son*—is buried there. Are you saying they won't let me bury Martin next to his daddy? We *own* that plot, Ephrum."

"The church reserves the right to deny interment. It's in all the papers."

"But they've never . . . how can they do this?"

"The deacons decide these things. Done by a proper vote."

"You're their chairman, Ephrum. What did you say to them on behalf of my son . . . on behalf of your own grandson?"

"It's been a hard thing on me, Liz. Has been on all of us. Don't make it any rougher."

She was standing now, the strength of her voice revealing an understanding that she now possessed an elusive dominion over the moment. She spoke slowly, raising her voice but maintaining restraint. "I want to know what you said to them about this. I want to know what you said to them about Martin."

"There wasn't nothing could be said. I've pledged my life to God's teachings. I'm bound to it. Martin turned away from the Word. Cast his lot with the ungodly. What am I supposed to say about that? I'm bound in the matter, Liz. Bound to follow God's law."

Laura had been looking on with shock, holding the outrage on her tongue until she could restrain it no more. "My *God*!" she shrieked. "I can't believe what I'm hearing. How can you say that?" Adam took her by the elbow and patted her forearm.

Slowly, the old man rose, his head bowed to the floor. Liz came around before him, stood directly in front of him. He looked up at her and their eyes locked in an unflagging exchange of energy and they stood face to face as if some impulse from the marrow of their bones were sustaining them. Liz spoke calmly and with certainty. "I want you out of my house. I want you to go now."

He did not answer, just turned in a protracted motion and walked into the wide hall toward the front door. They listened as the old hinges groaned open, then shut, and then he was gone.

Adam was the first to move, rising to approach Liz in a motion of compassion. But something he felt, some wraithlike barrier, arrested his step. The air in the kitchen was suddenly thick and stifling, and there was a sense of something ancient and distant settling into the present. They spread their gazes among each other's, each seeming to comprehend the other three as a single phenomenon, each feeling their own heart beating in harmony with the others. Liz spoke in a composed voice, the emotions of the past moments bleeding through in a slight, almost indiscernible vibrato. "Laura. Call Billups Funeral Home. Tell 'em we're moving the funeral to their chapel. See if they can do it tomorrow afternoon. Get us a time. We'll need to get a cemetery plot at Green Valley too. Ask 'em who we need to see about that." Then she turned and left the kitchen. Laura buried her head in her palms and began to sob. Adam reached for her arm.

* * *

They waited, all except for Jake, who kept watch at the house, the air woven with soft music and thick, sweet odors, mysterious odors of alien provenance. The table spread out before them in a business-like panel, supporting tired elbows and fatigued forearms. There was the promised arrival of the funeral director and there was slow-passing time, gradually assaulting the promise and threatening of its keeping.

Liz sat at the head of the table, rigid and dignified in her unadorned black dress, her face implacable, her hard-angled jaw locked in place. Laura watched her mother through misty eyes, a faint wheeze in her breath. Occasionally, she bit against her lower lip.

"What did you tell me about the cemetery, Laura?" her mother asked. "I'm sorry . . . I . . . I'm not remembering."

"Someone from Green Valley will be over to see us after we get the service arranged. We'll have to buy a plot. It won't be a problem."

"It's none of my business, of course," Adam said, "but it's better this way. That damn church . . . I don't understand how—"

"How can those bastards *do* this?" Laura interrupted. "It was *our family plot* for Christ sakes."

"*Laura*!" Her mother spoke sharply. "Calm yourself. We're not going to argue with them. We'll do it this way. He'll be buried just as proper. It'll still be a proper Christian burial."

"It will be a lot more *Christian* than anything that church has to offer," said Laura. "That's probably the last place Martin would want to be buried anyway."

"We won't talk no more about the church," Liz declared. "We'll just do what we've got to do."

Adam leaned forward. "We've never talked about this, Liz, but did Martin leave any instructions? A note or anything?"

She hesitated—met his eyes and looked away again, then spoke slowly. "There was a note."

Laura turned in shock. "You didn't tell me about a note, Mother."

"Wasn't important for you to know about it. Just cause more hurt."

"But I want to see it. I'm his sister and I want to see it."

"Fine. I'll show you. But let's get this over with first."

"Did he say anything about his burial?" Laura asked. Liz looked away.

"Well?" Laura insisted.

"Martin was a member of that church. Whatever else he might have done, he was a member of that church. What's proper is for him to be buried in the church cemetery."

"Which apparently is no longer an option," added Adam.

"Mother, does the note say anything about his wishes . . . about what he wanted done with his remains?"

She stared straight ahead, expressionless in the gathering uncertainty. Adam spoke to her firmly. "Liz, if Martin had anything to say about this, we need to know it now."

She looked first at Adam, then Laura. Then she stared at the opposite wall, focusing somewhere beyond the room, somewhere beyond the carefully arranged furnishings and objects surrounding them. At last she spoke. "He said he wanted to be cremated."

"What?" said Laura. "Mother, why didn't you *tell* us about this?"

Tears filmed Liz's eyes. "I don't know nothing about cremation," she said. "I don't like it . . . it's scary. Martin was a Christian. In spite of what them deacons say, he was a Christian. He deserves a Christian burial."

"But there's nothing unchristian about cremation. What gives you that idea?"

"It don't seem . . . I don't know . . . it don't seem Christian to me."

"Mother. Listen to me." She placed a hand on Liz's arm. "There's nothing unchristian about cremation. If this is what Martin wanted, then this is what we're going to do. We are going to abide by his wishes."

She began to sob, her voice cracking. "Ain't none of this right. We got our own family plot. Bought with good money. Your daddy's buried there. It ain't right I tell you. Martin was a Christian. I don't care what them deacons say, he was a Christian."

"Sure he was," said Laura.

"He deserves burying in that cemetery." She took a tissue from her purse and wiped her eyes. "Next to his daddy."

"And that we can't do," said Laura. "But what we can do is abide by his wishes. We are going to have him cremated, Mother. We are going to do what Martin wanted."

Liz composed herself. "You say it ain't . . . an unchristian thing to do?"

"No, Mother. It's not unchristian."

"And you, Adam. You agree it's the right thing?"

"I agree."

She shook her head slowly, as if she were swallowing a potent bitterness. "Then that's what we'll do. We'll do it the way he wanted."

The afternoon tired with them as they concluded their business and the sun was low in the sky when they left. It flickered at them through the trees as Adam drove, cast long shadows across the road. No one spoke. They drove by the church and through its massive shadow that blanketed the road and still no one spoke, all of them falling through the same silence, the same ponderous and malignant silence, all of them sinking inside it as if in quest of its source.

* * *

The bronze had begun an iron-like tarnishing, but it had been a year and six months and so that was to be expected—no surprise in it. It had sat untouched since his death, there on the parlor mantle, an unnatural provocation to the senses, resting next to a Limoges figurine that had been her grandmother's. At first, Liz had visited it daily, stood and contemplated it, maybe meditated, maybe prayed—she didn't know the difference anymore. A couple of months and the visits became less frequent. Her dwindling circle of friends eschewed the parlor, would not speak of it. Jake would sometimes stand there with her, hand upon her arm, no talking, their heads aswirl with hard-kept thoughts and memories. Then Jake found his own place and she was alone in the house—alone and lost in her own reflections. He dutifully visited with a good son's regularity. Sometimes they would walk in the yard, sometimes sit in the kitchen, small-talking the edge of their loss without mention of the front parlor or of that upon its mantle.

Laura had been down twice, providing what comfort a daughter could offer. Between visits, they spoke by telephone, the bond between them growing stronger in the wake of their loss and the expanding distance between Liz and the remnants of her old world. They found within each other an untapped strength, shared it in a symbiotic coupling of wounded caregivers, each giving and taking according to her needs and strengths.

Liz's relationship with Ephrum had been irreparably altered—cast into that vast space between vengeance and forgiveness where tolerance of his company was coldly permitted but genuine examination of the past was not. He had approached her a month after Martin's death, came to her humbly and urged her return to her regular Sunday pew. She heard him out, but declined, swore to him she would never again have anything to do with the Mount Shiloh Pentecostal Church. She walked away from it all, the years, the prayers, the sweat, the contributions of what money she could afford, walked away from everything she had ever invested in her own salvation, and the emptiness of that abandonment weighed on her like the misspent inheritance of a prodigal child. There were days when the loneliness rode too heavy against her and she longed to renew the lost relationships, longed to let the blood of bygone hurt ebb into the realm of the forgotten, but there was a limit to her capacity to forget.

By trial and error, she learned to endure the poisons her own mind randomly flung against her: her husband lying alone in his grave, her son, who should rightfully be resting beside him, reposing in an urn upon her mantle. She wondered if they were together now, Martin and his father. They should be, she thought. But things that had once been so clear had grown clouded. Stars that had once shone in pin-points of blue-white splendor were now diffused and blurred, undefined splotches of dim yellow against a murky sky. Her doubts grew as if in a culture beneath the quiet stillness of the house, and they hung there like the Spanish moss in the live oaks by the church cemetery.

In time, Laura became concerned with the stagnant course of her mother's life, and it tore at her to see a once strong vitality erode in the wash of loss that broke daily over her. It was as if she were waiting for life to finish with her—that she no longer had the capacity to direct the forces that set her agenda. And too, there was the issue that had lain dormant since the funeral, lingering like a curious ghost, that one and strangely uncomfortable question that no one had summoned the courage to ask aloud.

It was Laura who broached it, some marathon, late-night telephone conversation, each of them leaning hard into the other's loss, searching for sanctuary from their emptiness. Eighteen months and still there, and now it was time. And so it was Laura, the music of resolve in her head, leading her mother, just the way it had to be, the music swimming through her uncertainties, telling her it had to be, and her mother hearing it too, so chaste and innocent it had to be truth floating between them, mother and daughter, their passions coalescing into a singular purpose, a cocoon that sheltered them from the world's ambient noises and purified the song. The moonlight carried the music in a soft soprano and they were together within its melody, the music glissading between them like fireflies in a night breeze. Above them, the Spanish moss hung deep against the night and laid moonshadows among the quiet and cold tombstones. Standing now above his grave, she remembered it all, how he had three times planted life within her womb, remembered each of those three, each separate life she had borne and suckled and raised, clutched against her chest the remains of the one she had outlived. She held it there, a thing precious and enslaving, and Laura there too, the music between them clear in her head, and the stars like diamonds above them piercing the infinite night. She spun, arms extended, spun again as the weight in her hands fell away and the dust of her seed spread before her in swirling orbits, dancing on the wind like the trill of a flute, dancing inside the music and the sound of woman-laughter. And Laura with a hand against her, holding her as they spun together in the sublime certainty of the moment, touching as they spun, the weight disencumbering itself, her arms unburdened, the two standing now as one form among the stone monoliths, touching as she lowered her arms in release of all that she carried and had carried, and the music was free and unsullied, telling her it had to be, telling them both as they stood watching the wind carry away the dust, stir it across the stones and spread it over the ground of the Mt. Shiloh night.

# Annie McGill

I am not a man much affected by guilt. The tug of its gravity has never influenced my life's direction. Now I would not want you to think from this that I am without ethical principles or moral parameters. Quite the contrary. It is just that guilt is not the fuel that powers my quest for respectability. I've never had the time to wrestle with it. And I think I have been the stronger for it. No, I'll put it this way: I *know* I have been the stronger for it. It is a strength—I would even call it a freedom—that has served me well in what I do. It is an asset that I would not want to lose.

Whether my ability to skirt the reach of this most particularly human of all emotions is the chance of random genetics or the outcome of my upbringing is a matter of speculation. Was it my working-class background? Or the fact that I have always been more my father's son than my mother's boy? Don't try talking to me about oedipal complexes and repressed maternal attractions and psychobabble of that sort. That stuff means nothing to me—irrelevant riddles for which I have no patience. Did my mother exert some small influence on the courses I have plotted through my improbable life? Probably. Notwithstanding, I am, for better or worse, more of my father than I will dare admit when I can afford the luxury of an innocent dishonesty.

A 1960s Southern textile mill breeds a lot of hard men as it spins and weaves its cloth and my father was no differ-ent from the others. Too many underpaid hours in the heat and noise and hopelessness of a weave shed robs a man of his hearing and replaces it with a short temper and an unhealthy taste for liquor. I suffered through my share of the beatings—survived it all intact. I am, above all else, a survivor.

My mother survived too, though less successfully. Her answer to my father's rages was terrified submissiveness. That and her inexhaustible capacity to grant him the forgiveness that was never requested—that was accepted as a due like the redemption of a pawned thirty-eight—became the predictable cycle of their relationship. In another life, another social milieu, she could have been a woman of genteel grace and soft charm—serving mint juleps from silver trays, white gloves and that sort of thing. As it was, she was just one more haggard millwife fighting the daily grindingwheel of her existence, losing a little each day but hanging on . . . hanging on for reasons I could not begin to understand. Not then, not now—it is still unfathomable to me. The lessons that such an upbringing teaches cannot be learned from books. And they are lessons that, once learned, lie ponderously against memory, out of sight but always lurking, always ready to spring.

My mother had been dead ten years to the day when I first looked into the eyes of Annie McGill. Those who seek an order imposed by the positions of the stars and planets may find something more than a coincidence in that. Not that the two women bore any physical resemblance to each other, you understand. But there was an aura of pathos behind Annie's face—perhaps it was in the way she seemed to always be looking down into folded hands—that was reminiscent of mother, a look that lingered in the mind's eye after you turned away. Maybe I'm the only one who saw it, but then who but I would have known them both? Still, I'm positive that the similarity was real, certain that it was more than just a subjective feeling peculiar to me, even though I've found it impossible to articulate. Just a hint of an aura that hovered above them, like some short riff from a guitar recalling a forgotten melody from a past place and time. Something that lingers after you turn away.

Don't think for a minute that I am complaining about the cruel nature of my upbringing. The same fortune that dealt me familial dysfunction also endowed me with a vision to see beyond the horizons where my childhood peers and social superiors fixed their own shortsighted gazes. I had certain abilities that served me well in those years—that serve me well today. There was that uncanny knack of consistently posting high scores on the achievement tests—"testing well," they called it. And of more practical application at the time was the music. The first time I picked up a guitar I could sense it—that feeling of control that, for most musicians, comes only with a certain level of mastery over the instrument. But a natural feels the power with the first touch, and conquest of the technical aspects of musicianship is simply a matter of the fingers catching up with the mind and spirit.

The raw desperation of the blues, its ribald poetry and unadorned pleadings, quickly became my master. It was as though the guitar had reached within me and seized some dormant emotion, grabbed it and launched it in a new direction. Willie Dixon, Elmore James, then Clapton—I listened to them all, digested their music and played it back through the filter of my own soul. I claimed it for myself and made it my own. By the time I'd graduated high school, I had my choice of bands to sign on with.

Never being one to close off options, I lived that part of my life in a series of short-term commitments. The music became more for me than just an end unto itself—it was a meal ticket that saw me through four years of college and three more of law school. Sure, it was a fast life, bouncing from late night gigs at small bars, to the beds of those women who inevitably congregate around the passing of the after-the-show cokespoon, and then, to the law books. An incongruous existence to be sure, but unlike most of my new compatriots, I had no set of external expectations to live up to—no lofty professional goals that others were pushing me to attain. I was free to deviate from the straightjacket of congruity. I even held open the possibility of making music my full-time career, but despite several studio gigs in Memphis and Nashville, nothing ever came together for me on a truly professional level. And my mindset at the time was to ride with the current—no need to try shaping my own fate. That current had, after all, brought me a long way from my source and I was generally satisfied with the direction of its flow. Why would I have wanted to buck the trend?

But that is old history now and there are more than a score of years between my darker past and the day that I, as a prominent and successful criminal defense attorney, first looked upon the face of Annie McGill. It was in district court, a preliminary hearing in the Malcomb Carsden case. The bruises in the photographs were gone, but hers was still very much the face of a victim. I remember her sitting there at the state's table with the victim's services officer, an older heavyset woman with goggled eyesockets set deeply into a frog-like face that flashed anger with each gaze in my direction. And Annie, her bobbed black hair precisely contoured to the creamy roundness of her face and those eyes that were so vulnerable and pleading, the pupils and irises melding into a single shade of darkness. Too helpless to ever be taken seriously—too soft to challenge a man like me.

Some would think the journey from my beginnings to that courtroom a most improbable circumstance. In fact, it was as natural as the beat of a hummingbird's wings. When I say that I am good at what I do, I do not mean this at all in a boastful way. I was simply born with a natural proclivity to persuade. I did nothing to earn it or deserve it, it just happened that way. That ability, together with a good dose of unflagging doggedness, carried me through the bare, early years. My first clients were people who had no choices—the moneyless hoard of criminally accused indigents. People who have the luxury of choice don't hire lawyers in storefront offices sparsely furnished and smelling of secondhand vinyl. I accepted the realities of my position, hustled for the appointments knowing better times would come. It did not bother me, starting at the bottom of the legal food chain. I was used to living scantly and without the respect of polite society. I garnered enough income over the first couple of years to take care of the overhead and provide modest amounts of food and shelter. Juggling a few credit cards allowed for the clothing.

It didn't take the tight-assed pretty boys and girls in the district attorney's office long to discover my courtroom savvy. Not after I'd kicked them around a few times, winning acquittals in cases where they should have slam-dunked me. The district attorney took notice too, and soon I was going up against his most experienced prosecutors. They fared little better against me. Something about standing before a jury was, for me, like picking up a guitar. I had that same feeling of assuredness and control that I used to get when I put the strap across my shoulder and felt the frets under my fingers. I worked the juries like the strings of the instrument. I knew instinctively where they wanted to go and how to take them there—and how to leave them with that one lingering reasonable doubt about my client's guilt when the facts seemed so undeniably certain on the surface. I was their trusted boatman, ferrying them through the currents and eddies of the case and landing them, more often than not, just where I wanted.

"You thrive on the feeling of power you get from this, don't you," the district attorney said to me once as we waited for the jury in a particularly difficult murder case. It was not posed as a question.

"Funny you should be the one asking that," I replied. "Where is there more power than in the hands of one who decides whether to prosecute a fellow citizen?"

"Maybe in the hands of one who has more than his fair share of ability to control the prosecution's outcome."

"Better for my clients that I control it rather than you."

"You ought to inventory your clients . . . reflect on who it is you're wasting your talents on." He glared at me as if he thought he had some magical capacity to read or even sway me. He had no idea how hollow his futile words rang. Our eyes locked in a combative stare, no one speaking, no one flinching. When he finally turned away, he knew who of us was the stronger—the greater survivor. I don't recall him ever speaking to me again.

After several years at the bottom of the legal hierarchy, I began my climb. I never pressed things—I have never been into self-promotion, so maybe it took longer than it might have—but after you win enough acquittals, even with the indigent appointments, word gets around. So when Dr. Rhinemon's daughter got busted with a little coke in her purse, the good doctor's prominent uptown lawyer, who didn't dirty his own hands with the criminal work, knew who to call. Then there was the corruption trial of a city councilman and a few nightly appearances on the six o'clock news. Eventually, I began to get referrals from the large, prestigious firms. A partner's son stopped for drunk driving, an important client's wife caught embezzling from the church till—they all came knocking. And the endless proliferation of illegal drugs helped to generate a steady flow of business. They got good service from me—the best I had to give them. Even when I lost a case (and there were some losses—no one wins them all) my clients knew they'd gotten their money's worth. They knew that no one would ever again show them such loyalty and fight for them with such savage purpose. It is a principle of mine that my clients get everything they pay me for and more. It is a principle that I never violate.

As I moved from the appointed cases to the paying clients, I quickly learned how easy it was to separate desperate people from their money. When you're selling hope to the hopeless, people don't quibble about the cost. Once the well-moneyed clients started to find my door, my lifestyle began to change—nicer car, a house and mortgage, a small farm to retreat to. After my father drank himself to death, I even helped my mother out a little. She would never have asked for it, but she accepted my assistance graciously.

And of course, there were the women—a different breed from the girls I'd been with as a youth and a struggling lawyer. I became adept at spotting them—women with money to spend and a hunger in need of fulfillment. The ones from failing marriages were the easiest prey. Like me, they were anxious to strike a short-term bargain with an acceptable partner. Now I was acceptable and always, always ready to deal.

My sudden access to money did not change me in any significant respect. Sure, I loved having it, loved the freedom and entrée it bought me, but it never became my master. I have always viewed money as merely a useful byproduct of my work. Being slave to neither money nor guilt keeps the head clear and the goal in sharp focus. So when Malcomb Carsden, the son of real estate mogul Nate Carsden, appeared in my office with a briefcase full of neatly stacked hundred-dollar bills, it was his story I first wanted. The money was a secondary concern.

Malcomb was, without a doubt, one of the stranger birds I have ever called a client—walking proof that wealth cannot purchase normality. His skin glowed with that creamy tanning-bed bronze of the affluent. His baby-smooth face bore a texture that suggested he was incapable of growing facial hair. The blue eyes were spaced too closely above a narrow, pointed nose, and they sparked with a mocking gleam. He could not have been more than twenty-five.

"I need to hire a lawyer," he said, opening the briefcase and flashing its contents at me. "I hear you're the best." I sat unmoved, ignoring the money, focusing on his skewed smile and the thick shocks of dark blond hair that framed his face down to his shoulders.

"You're in some sort of trouble then," I said in a deliberately distant voice.

"I've been arrested. Rape and attempted murder." He held his mouth slightly opened, the trace of a smile still bent into his lips. "But I didn't do it. I swear."

"I didn't ask you if you did it," I said. I never ask. It is something I do not need to know.

"The girl they say I raped . . . she was beaten badly. The paper said she told the police she couldn't remember anything. She couldn't pick me out of the police line-up either."

"So why'd they arrest you?"

"Old lady Stiggers. The senile old crone across the hall from the girl's apartment. She told the police she saw me leaving there the night it happened."

"Did she?"

"No way!"

"And this Miss Stiggers—had she seen you before?"

"My eleventh-grade history teacher. She's addled as a shithouse mouse."

"What about the girl? Did you know her?"

"Never laid eyes on her. Even to this day."

"You prepared to hire me?"

"They say money talks and bullshit walks. This ain't bullshit in this briefcase."

"How much you got there?"

"Thirty-thousand. I can get more if you need it."

I took his case and his thirty-thousand. That afternoon I spent learning all I could about Annie McGill. Information is power, and with the network of sources I had put together, I was a powerful man. Annie, I learned, had been eking out a subsistence as a hairdresser. She and her live-in boyfriend had just split up—he'd moved out two weeks before the attack and hadn't been seen since. He became my investigator's first assignment.

I tried contacting Miss Stiggers but she wouldn't see me. The police had already told her to keep quiet. The only bone the cops threw me was a private viewing of the pictures they'd taken of Annie after the attack. A thick-fingered policeman with a crew cut and sweating forearms sat with me at a small table in a mildewed basement stacked high with boxes, and fumbled through the harrowing pictures as if he were dealing a hand of stud poker. They showed a brutally beaten young girl, the soft lines of her face a stark contrast to the deep purple coloration around the eyes. The look was expressionless, betraying nothing. "Thisiz thuh profile shot . . . showing thuh bruise to thuh left temple," he mumbled clinically between heavy breaths, handing me another photograph. I noticed how he watched me as I studied the pictures and how he always looked away whenever I tried to meet his eye.

The preliminary hearing was my first chance to size up the witness, Miss Stiggers. She was the grandmotherly type, gray hair up in a bun, a bit of superfluous skin dangling from the face and arms. Potentially, a very dangerous witness. I approached her with a gentle cautiousness, probing her with no trace of attack in my questions. I measured her like a tailor, noting every nuance in her voice, each hesitancy in her speech. When I'd finished with my cross-examination, I was confident I could destroy her at trial.

But there was something odd about that hearing that has taken up residence within me—a sensation I experienced as I worked through the old lady's testimony. I don't put much stock in paranormal phenomena, ESP and that sort of stuff, but I felt those eyes leaning against my back—Annie's eyes, I was sure they were—felt their icy prickle as true and corporal as a hammer against my thumb. For a nanosecond, I was distracted. I looked around and saw that frozen, hungerless face, devoid of anger, bereft of emotion, the satiny, dark-velvet eyes at its center ready to swallow me into some parallel universe, one where she held all the cards and called the game. No, I was not going to be taken to such a place. The idea of it was as absurd then as it is now. Still it was an intense and ephemeral experience—like being on a threshold of a great conflict and being pulled in opposite directions by unrecognizable forces. I looked away from her quickly, redirecting my focus on the witness. The chill in my back faded, then went away altogether, but the memory of that moment haunts me yet. It infects my dreams and thrusts the indelible face into my consciousness at random and unexpected intervals. Then it dissipates like a melting apparition and I feel the chill of a girl's stare lingering upon me—lingering after I look away.

Over the next four months, I immersed my life in the case. I felt myself driven by a compulsion I had never before experienced, as if my own survival were somehow linked to Malcomb Carsden's fate. No lead was too remote to follow, no trail too irrelevant to explore. My investigator finally found Annie's lost boyfriend living in another state and we dug up enough dirt on him to make a compelling argument that he was capable of the grotesque act of violence committed against her. Then I turned to the preliminary hearing transcripts, dissected them, memorized the weaknesses in the Stiggers testimony and planned the decisive ambush I would execute at trial. And I worked . . . and worked . . . with Malcomb.

It was not that Malcomb was dense or slow to learn. He had a keen enough mind and was quick on the uptake. The problem was his facial expressions and body language, things jurors pick up on subconsciously that have as much impact as the facts themselves: the smirky, spoiled-kid way he twisted his mouth, his cavalier gestures. I was not concerned about preparing him to testify—I was not going to let him near the witness stand—but I knew the jury would watch his reactions to the other witnesses. I had to recreate his mannerisms and revamp his casual indifference, otherwise my case was lost. It took great patience, but by the trial date, I had reinvented Malcomb Carsden. I watched him in my periphery as the state's witnesses testified. And I knew as I watched his even-tempered and understated display of emotion that his acquittal was won. It was only left for me to destroy the state's key witness, Miss Stiggers. I accomplished it with a gentle hand and condescending tone—no aggressive attack for the grandmother. When I was done with her, the prosecution's case was shambles. As she stepped down from the stand, I turned to the trio of prosecutors, their heads all buried in documents that they only pretended to read. Annie sat in the middle of them facing straight ahead like a sphinx, her eyes focused on nothing, her hands folded on the table in front of her. I watched the muscles of her neck twitch and her head slowly revolve toward me. Before her gaze could catch me, I looked toward Malcomb. His demure countenance mimicked precisely that of an innocent man. I thought about how well I had taught him and how well he had learned. Then I felt it again, that iciness against the back of my head, and I knew that Annie was looking at me.

Even at the close of the most well-tried case, there is an element of the unknown as the jury deliberates. I watched it in Malcomb as he sat alone in the hallway outside the courtroom, waiting for the jury. The late afternoon sun threw long quadrilaterals of golden light through the panes of the westward-facing windows, and a terrified, rising anxiety seemed to spin from the hall floor and become nearly visible in the golden rays. I stood out of the field of his peripheral sight, studying him in the dying light. He looked so small seated there on the wooden bench beneath the high ceiling and within the vast width of the hallway. He bore an appearance I had not seen in him before—the look of true terror. In another person, it might have been a vision that evoked pity in me, but for Malcomb, I felt nothing of that. It was an almost satisfying sensation to see him sitting there, waiting in his extreme and fearful uncertainty. For how long I watched him, I could not tell you. We were both in that state where the mind does not find it necessary to mark the passage of time. My trance was broken when he suddenly looked up at me. The sun caught his tanned face at a strange, unnatural angle and the native blueness of his eyes was muted in the autumn light. He did not speak or even acknowledge my presence and he looked away as quickly as he had thrown his gaze upon me. But something in the way he slid his eyes away from me, in the carriage of his head and the cock of his brow, or maybe it was the slow movement of his tongue over his upper lip, revealed all of his secrets. In that one instant he erased the few weak doubts I still held, and I felt a loathing for him such as I had never felt before toward anyone I'd ever called a client. I walked away and left him alone, silhouetted against the window and the dying afternoon beyond.

Twenty miles from my office, hidden within twisting ribbons of slag-topped county roads, is the small farm I bought years ago when I began to derive more income from my profession than I had immediate need of. It has a modest, ill-maintained house that serves me well enough as a retreat from the work it has become my fate to pursue. I often go there for regeneration after a particularly strenuous battle. After the jury acquitted Malcomb Carsden, I went there for a week. My favorite time is in the late fall when a few determined leaves still cling to the poplars and red oaks and the crimson sumac stands brilliant against the dead-straw brush. There is a red-tail hawk that nests on a ridge at the edge of my land. If you are watching when the hunger rises in her, you might see her circle the dead and cutover field, circling until she finds it, some small perturbation in the underbrush, and sets her sights upon the prey. She will flow on the breeze as if she were within it—a part of it and it a part of her. She is as a vessel sailing through the primordial ether, never faltering through the uneven gusts and updrafts, riding each shift in course and intensity as if she knows the very mind of the wind. Finally she will dive, the totality of her consciousness focused upon the prey, answering to voices of unreckonable age that echo through her veins and sculpt every nuance of her wingform. With talons outstretched, she will close on her objective until in one blinding explosion of time and space and swirling dust, she will complete what nature demands of her in exchange for survival. She has no time for remorse. The bargain she has made with nature does not admit of guilt. Unlike the vultures that bat their clumsy, poaching wings over the stench of roadkill, she will eat only what she kills. She is strong and noble and, above all, she endures. It is a source of strength for me to watch her hunt—to see her in all of the rawness of her survival. On many cold November mornings, I have risen at dawn to partake of this communion. On mornings when the air is pregnant with moisture, the mists will rise off the creek and spread through the field and rob the eyes of their distance. When the fog grows dense, the eyes will play tricks on the mind. I have been in the field on such mornings, breathed the thick air and looked into the myth-laden dawn, seen things I knew were not there—faces from the past that are no longer real. Now, when I look into those fogs, I look with hope and fear, and I hold my breath, for I know that the face of Annie McGill is somewhere within the mist, and I know that if it appears, the hawk will not come.

# Slocomb's Money

## *Slocomb*

So here comes Prescott easing down my walk like a slide of mud, July sweat leaking down them jowls, him in a black three-piece, vest stretched like onionskin across his belly, stepping on all the cracks like it don't mean nothing and mashing the crabapples to the cement like purple wads of something dead, and me watching through the window by the fan and Longjohn barking at him through the yardweeds like the devil hisself done come to call. He starts up the steps, goes to hammering the screen door, "Slocomb, I know you're there," looking back at Longjohn like he's knowing he don't bite, but yet again ain't quite sure, and yelling, "come to the door goddamnit," and Longjohn barking and growling like he's done hemmed up Satan. I stay quiet, watching Opra talking to some highfalutin San Francisco sweetboy, trying to listen over all the damn barking and banging and the fan whirring faster than Brandi's tongue when she's agitated, which is most of the time here lately. Then he opens the screen and comes up on the porch like it's his to begin with, stirring through all them plugs of floordust and last spring's pollen, and goes to pounding the front door and fixing to come around in just a second and peek through the window to where he can see me lying on the couch.

"Alright," I says. "Hold ya goddamn hosses," I says, knowing he's gon' keep banging till I get the door open, and Longjohn still going at him like he's coughing up brimstone. "Whas got you out this morning?" I says to him, knowing full well the reason, and he goes to raking them big hands over hisself like he thinks he's done got them fine clothes all dirty.

"You never brought me that policy, Slocomb. I figured you forgot about it and I was in the neighborhood, so . . ." And I can't breathe a good breath without sucking up the fumes of that damn cologne he spills all over hisself, trying to cover up what-all smells them hands has took up in a lifetime of handling the dead. "I figured you just forgot me," he says, and him knowing that it ain't no truth in it and that I ain't really forgot nothing. "So I was over this way and thought I'd come by and pick up that policy. Save you the trouble."

"I'd done forgot about it," I lied. "Lemme go look."

"*Look for it*? Hell, you had it with you the other day. Right there in my office you had it. Where you got to look for it at? You ain't lost it that quick."

"I put it back for safekeeping," I told him. "I think I throwed it in this box here," and I go pick up a box of Callie's papers from off the floor behind the couch and set it on the dining table in the next room, right on top of the strowed about pieces of the puzzle Brandi brought over and my half-together, headless Statue of Liberty, and I go to fumbling through papers like I'm looking for that damn insurance policy I had to show him before he'd bury her proper. "I thought I throwed the damn thing in here," I lied. "And now I can't find it. But I know it's around here somewheres."

"Around here my ass," he says. "You slippery son of a bitch. You think I don't know what you're up to?"

"And that'd be what?" I says, looking back towards him with mean in my eye.

"That'd be you slipping that damn policy back outta my file the minute I turned my head."

"All I can figure is it musta somehow come to get mixed up with my own papers and I picked it up by mistake."

"*Bullshit*!" he bellows. "I bet you've done cashed it in and got the money stashed somewhere."

"Accuse me of such dishonesty in my own house will you, Prescott?" I says to him in my maddest voice. "I know it's right here somewheres, if you'll just hold your—"

"I want my money, Slocomb," he says. "My five thousand dollars, or by God I'll dig'er up," and him glaring at me like some humongous goblin dressed in black, face soaking and bulging and shaking like a wild hog. "I'moan dig'er up'n leave'er on your goddamn porch."

"You'd do it too, you heartless son of a bitch," I says, knowing full well he wouldn't. "A pore disabled brick mason, a most honorable white man, done lost his wife and you'd treat me no better'n a spent-out panhandler."

"You ain't worth killing, Slocomb," he says. "If you was, I'd do it myself. You get me that money or I'll damn sure dig'er up and then you can get rid of her best you can." And then he waddles off, creaking the porch floor with his fat, cussing most unpolitely at Longjohn in the yard where he's heaving at the chest and growling low and serious and teeth shining like chisels and Prescott's looking back like he ain't afraid, but he'll watch him just the same, and Longjohn follows him to the gate and he shuts it on him and turns back to cuss him some more, louder and more spiteful this time, and then brushes off them fine clothes and climbs into his Lincoln and spins his tires and off down the street he goes.

## *Brandi*

It's what Mama would'a wanted. An opportunity. A chance for the betterment of the family.

"But what about Karl?" he says to me. "He'll aim at claiming his fair half of it. Even if I don't keep none of it myself, Karl'll aim to get his half. And Prescott's wanting to get paid out of it. What am I gone do about him?"

And what's Karl gonna do with it but suck it up his nose in a month's time? And Prescott . . . that fat son of a bitch can go piss in the quarry. He don't need it, setting up there in his big showhouse with more money than God. But a flower shop, now that's an idea. And ten thousand dollars and a mortgage and I'm in business and he'll get paid back in three years, maybe two if things goes right. And with interest. It's a chance for the betterment of the family, I say.

So first Karl's got to be dealt out, 'cause half of ten thousand ain't near enough. Prescott I'll tackle later.

When I get to his trailer, the usual hoodlums ain't about, except for one runny-nosed, over-tattooed tee shirt that looks like he's been on a six week fast. He's stumbling towards a red Maverick, crunched fender and all, looking back over his shoulder at me, distrustful, like he can't get away fast enough, dragging the back of his hand under his leaky nostril. I check the wire between my boobs while the tee shirt tries to crank his junk heap. Still where Sergeant Darwin taped it. He's had lots of experience with these things. Or so he tells me. Lots of experience handling tits is more like it. The tee shirt tries the ignition for the fifth time. Finally, success. He revs the motor until it backfires loud as a twelve-gauge.

Karl's sitting cross-legged on the waterbed in the corner, the room dark from the sheet hung over the window—a tie-dyed penis-tip purple. His eyes are hollow as the world. "You seen Hat Daddy yet?" I ask, and he nods me a fat smile. "Let's see it then," I say, and he gets out the mirror and razor blade and we both do a line and it ain't too bad either. I pay him with the special bills, thinking how fast could this worthless slug piss away five thousand dollars and what a waste it'd be and I'd never swing the flower shop then.

Sgt. Darwin nods at me when I drive by where he's pulled over in the bushes. Now they'll go in there with a search warrant and Karl'll be caught as an infield pop-up. And never know how, never'll think it was me. Do I feel bad about it? Maybe a little, but there's times when you got to look beyond your own feelings. Like now. Because it's for the betterment of the family. What Mama woulda wanted.

Next day I drive up and Daddy's standing in the yard, feeding tablescraps to Longjohn. If he's gonna wear them skimpy undershirts, I wish he'd at least shave his pits.

"I think Karl's in some kind of trouble," I tell him and take the cool spot by the fan. "The police was out at his trailer. Cars of 'em, crawling around thick as cane syrup. I reckon they've finally done caught up with him and his nose candy. It ain't surprising."

"Lord, Godamighty," he moans. "I knowed it was bound to happen sooner or later. But what could I do. And this on top of everything else. I'm a cursed man, I tell you."

"You can't give him that money now," I say. "He won't have no need of it where he's headed."

"I tried to lead that boy straight. But would he listen to me? Naw, because he already knowed it all. And now this. And on top of everything else."

"On top of what else?" I ask.

"Them papers the sheriff brought by," he says, and points to the dining room table. "Prescott's done sued me for the funeral bill."

Sure enough, there it is, all official-looking and signed by His High-and-Mightiness, Mr. T. Stanley Bueron, attorney-at-law, lying right where the Statue of Liberty's head ought to be if he'd ever finish putting together that goddamn puzzle I bought him while Mama was in the hospital. "What you gonna do about this?" I ask.

"There ain't nothing to do but pay him. I got to take that insurance money and settle up."

"The hell you have," I say. "You got to find a way to put him off. I can't swing the flower shop on nothing less than the full ten thousand. Prescott's gonna have to wait."

"Them papers don't say nothing about him wanting to wait."

"I'll handle this," I tell him, gathering up the papers. "I gotta lawyer I'll let look at it. All we need's a little time. Once I get the shop open and running I can start making payments."

"I'm a cursed man, I tell you," he whines.

"Just shut up and get me the goddamn money." He's lost it now. I know he needs me to take charge.

"The money's safe," he says. "And I ain't decided what I want to do with it."

I argue with him, but he won't move. "It's safe," he keeps saying. A hundred Franklins stuffed in a can somewhere and he says it's safe. So I got to give him more line—play him like a trophy large-mouth until he's ready to be reeled up. Until he can see what's best for the family.

## *Bueron*

I suppose it was Winston Prescott who first opened my eyes to the lucre attainable through the commerce of human dispatchment. It's not surprising really—the fact that undertaking can be such a comfortably remunerative profession. It is, after all, a service that we all come to need sooner or later. And Winston, while he may be thought coarse and common, is the consummate disciple of Adam Smith. He simply recognized the natural inelasticity of a particular demand and stepped forward to supply the market. A savvy economic analyst with a natural proclivity for separating the grieving and vulnerable from their money. A monument to American capitalism.

It was an absorbing journey to watch, his rise from son of an auto mechanic and a sewing-room seamstress to one of the ten largest landowners in Bedford County, Alabama. His parents were a decent, humble sort, always wanting the best for their only child. I remember their honest nervousness when they came to me for their wills—probably the only occasion they'd ever had to be in a lawyer's office. They died within six months of each other, when Winston was in his early twenties, leaving him a 1200-square-foot woodframe on a street of 1200-square-foot woodframes and a few thousand in the bank. I probated the wills and he's been a client ever since. Small things mostly, and always the haggle over fees. I should have fobbed him off on a younger lawyer years ago, one hungry enough to put up with his aggressive cost-control tactics. But we seem irrevocably bonded to each other, Winston and I, bound by a wicked inertia to continue our trek together, albeit at a good arm's distance.

I confess to a secret amusement upon hearing his account of how "Snake" Slocomb bamboozled him out of a funeral—brought in the insurance policy and then nicked it back out of the file while Winston was typing the obituary. Still a little agility left in those callused brick-mason hands. There aren't many who could have taken Winston in that way, but if there's one thing "Snake" Slocomb ever did come by honestly, it's his nickname.

Joan buzzes to tell me he's in the waiting room with his daughter—Brandi, I believe her name is. I tell her to offer them coffee and have them wait in the conference room. Winston rattles his throat clear, reaches over my desk for a Kleenex. "I want you to tell that thieving son of a bitch we're gonna put him where they'll have to pipe in sunlight," he growls.

"Just let me handle it, Winston," I tell him. "If he's not cashed the policy yet, we're okay. We can garnish the proceeds directly from the company."

He wipes the Kleenex across his mouth. "And if he *has* cashed it?"

I pause, tap a pencil against my knee. "Ever try to get honey from a wasp nest?"

He bangs a fist against the desk corner, rattling the disarray that overspreads it, and prattles on about steel bars and piped-in sunlight.

The Snake is plainly ill at ease in my conference room. He waits apprehensively, his eyes scouring the bookshelves. His fingers fidget. The daughter is quite his opposite, sitting erect, confident, even arrogant, ready to transact business, obviously unruffled at the turpitude surrounding her father's position.

"I am hopeful that we can resolve this dispute today," I begin, addressing the daughter. "And save ourselves the . . . inconvenience of a court appearance." She has not spared the application of her best cologne. A hint of peach in there, if I'm not mistaken.

"He don't have the money," she says. "We'll have to set up payments. Take care of it by the month."

"What'd he do with it, then?" demands Prescott. "Give it to you for safekeeping?"

"None of your damn business what he done with it," she says. "That policy was made out to him. You'll get paid in time."

"And we'll find you a cell right between his thieving ass and your drug-dealing brother," says Prescott. "Your whole worthless family locked all in a row." He has the look of one come early to grab the best seat at a public hanging.

There is standing, shouting, name calling, Brandi's aggressively raised middle finger. I quickly usher Winston from the room. When I return, Slocomb's elbows are propped on the table, his head buried dolefully in his hands. Brandi paces the floor, her lips testing a freshly lit cigarette.
"So what are y'all gonna do about it?" she asks.

"I don't allow smoking in here," I say.

She snuffs out the cigarette in a glass coaster. I suppose she *could* have mistaken it for an ashtray, but I have doubts. "I'll sign a note," she says. "Pay it back in installments."

"We can't agree to that," I say. "Either pay up now or we go on to court. And I don't think your father wants to have to explain to Judge Adamson how he fished that policy out of Mr. Prescott's file. It's in his best interest . . . and yours too . . . to bring me that money."

From the moment I first watched her sitting there next to the Snake, I knew she wouldn't be intimidated. Her implacable self-assurance, the jaw angled out like a dare, the acidic squint in her eye—it all said *we're keeping this money.* There was one solitary strong point to Slocomb's position, and she recognized it and milked it for all its value—that tired old bromide: possession is nine-tenths of the law. She was not going to be separated from her father's windfall by something so trite as notions of right and wrong. I thought of Prescott as I watched her, how the two of them were fired in the same kiln. They were—how can I put it?—not two souls who'd lost their innocence (because you can't lose what you never had) but two congenital non-innocents, one foraging for comforts not much beyond mere survival, the other for a surplus he would never have need to tap, both plunging headlong into life with a surfeit of truculence and a dearth of virtue. Their conflict was, as I say, a source of perverse amusement to me. Prescott, of course, was right in the matter and there was no question of our ultimate success in the case, but the law (resolving disputes, as it does, one case at a time) has never been a scale on which to weigh one's long-term ethical worth. And so a lifetime of oblique deceptions does not, at least in the eyes of blind justice, overbalance the mass of a simple outright theft.

It soon became evident that compromise with Brandi was hopeless. We argued, she yelled, Slocomb sunk his head deeper against the table, arms overlocked like a giant forlorn mollusk. Winston waited in my office, no doubt stewing in fantasies of vengeance and retribution: the entire family sodomized in their cells by three-hundred-pound Neanderthals, or slow-roasted by hooded torturers in a medieval dungeon. Justice is such a subjective commodity, always so much more satisfying when meted out by the imagination.

## *Brandi*

Hat Daddy digs lazy in his big nose, your basic thumb-picker, the sunset blazing behind him, pulsing like an erupting volcano, and his glasses like two black windows in the glowing lava. I see in those windows the reflection of spongy dice dangling from the rearview mirror. "A runny-nosed bastard in a beat-up Maverick," I say. "Had to been him. No other explanation." The dice show a hard eight.

"Hmmm," says Hat Daddy in a rattling baritone. He rubs his thumb over his tight-jeaned thigh. "Sho do look like dangerous weather."

"You gonna need help now that Karl's going off. I been back to the trailer. Got his list. Lucky the cops didn't find it. All the old contacts on it. You gonna need help with 'em."

"And you think you be the one?"

"Oh yeah. At least you know you can trust me. Who else can you say that about?"

He smiles, reaches in his breast pocket for a cigarette, hands me one too, then lights them both. "Time to lay low for awhile. Things gone be too hot."

"Not for them that's careful," I say. "Just front me one ounce. I'll have it all sold by the weekend."

Smoke rises before his face. His teeth are too white, shimmering. The sky behind him burns orange. "You fucking outcho mind."

"One ounce. I'll get you paid back by the weekend."

He sucks on the cigarette, holds it in, calculates, his

smile broadens. "Meet me behind Skipper's. Nine tonight."

"You got it," I say. "I'm there."

He flicks an ash into the lava, his teeth growing longer, brighter. "You fucking out'cho mind."

Now I'm dialing the phone, standing next to Jarred who's got no idea. Other than he thinks he's about to get lucky. I always said an ex-boyfriend's as useless as chicken shit to a poultry farmer. But his voice does have that uncanny resemblance to Karl's. Use the things the Lord provides you, I say, or don't blame others for your misery.

When I get a ring, I hand him the phone. We've been over this ten times, but if there's a way to screw it up, Jarred'll find it. But that voice of his—so much like Karl's, it could fool even me.

"Mr. Prescott, please," he says to the receiver. "Tell him it's Karl Slocomb."

There's a long pause. Then he begins again. "I'm calling from jail and I gotta make this quick. My goddamn sister set me up. I need bail money. I'll tell you where the insurance money is if you'll help me." There's a pause while the fish surveys the bait. Then he goes on. "She give it to a friend to keep. She's getting it back from him tonight at nine. Meeting him behind Skipper's Place on Carlisle Street. He's a big black guy, goes by the name Hat Daddy. It'll be wrapped in a brown paper package."

Yeah, I hate it that Hat Daddy's got to go down too. But to get Prescott, ain't that worth it? Besides, Hat's been off before—he knows how to cope on the inside. But Prescott, he's primed for one hell of a fall. Fixing to get served up all of what he deserves plus a big second helping. Sorry about it all, Hat. When this is over with, I'll send you a bowl of daisies. I wonder if they let 'em keep flowers in a prison dorm.

Sgt. Darwin can't believe what he's hearing. He's dragging his palm across his forehead, eyes about to explode outta the sockets. "Winston Fucking Prescott . . . ." He stretches it out, savoring the pleasure of each syllable. "Why is it I'm not surprised?"

"It's going down behind Skipper's Place. Look for the brown package. Tell your boys they better not screw this one up."

"Winston Fucking Prescott," he says shaking his head from side to side, smiling like a preacher counting collection.

We argue all the time now, me and Daddy. He don't understand the benefits of me owning a business. "That money's put safe away," he says. "I still ain't decided about it." I know he's worried about Prescott and his lawsuit. When that's out of the way, things'll get clearer. What else will there be left to do with it? What else but a flower shop?

"Finished the puzzle, I see," I shout to him in the kitchen, where he's gone to get a beer. I need to change the subject before this thing boils too far over.

"'Cept for that missing piece," he says. There's a hole right in the middle of Liberty's green face where the table shows through. "It's fell off on the floor somehow and got itself lost. I got to crawl around and look for it."

"I'd help you, but I got to be going. I got to get ready for an important meeting tonight."

"About that damn flower shop, I reckon," he says.

"You might say that," I say going out the door. "You could very well say it's about that."

Sgt. Darwin's wired me again, but I've disconnected it this time. He don't need to hear any conversation that's going to confuse him. I'll tell him it come undone by accident.

I get there first and wait for Hat. The lot's full of parked cars, but Prescott's Lincoln ain't around, but he wouldn't of brought that anyway—he'd be afraid I'd recognize it. But no doubt he's hunkered down in one of the others, waiting. Hat's late, but that ain't unusual. But it does fray my nerves a bit. This ain't the kind of thing a body does every day.

Finally he shows. He gets out of his car, backlit by a gauzy streetlight, and I see the outline of his showy hat and walk towards him. He's got the package and my heart's racing faster than I can remember. What if Prescott don't come? What if Hat Daddy goes down for nothing? Things it's too late to worry about teasing my mind. Then I hear footsteps coming at me from behind and I know it's all right. Hat gets this look on his face like *what the fuck's going down*? I take the package and turn and there's Prescott. All I have to do is stick it out to him and he grabs it out of my hands faster than a bum reaching for a pint bottle. Then I can see in his face that he knows it's all wrong. Because I handed it over too easy. Because it ain't the right weight to be money. I smile at him to tell him he's right, to tell him he's fucked. Then the commotion starts: Hat Daddy running, men coming out of the bushes with guns yelling *get down*, spotlights busting over the lot, a gunshot exploding, and Prescott's standing there froze with that package, mouth open like a big carp, and his mind ain't quite caught up with it all, but he's getting closer and by the time they put the cuffs on him, he's gonna just about have it all worked out. Yeah, he'll whine about being set up, but let him whine on. They ain't gonna believe him, especially when they search his big Lincoln and find the dime bag under the floormat. You really ought to of locked your car, Winston Fucking Prescott.

## *Slocomb*

The water's moving under me, flinging the sun up in my eyes and I have to squint like when you're fishing and your cork floats into the light. The big boat plows through the water like a tractor over a rolling field, up and down, a real slow up and down, and the wind and spray whooshing over my face, cleaning me, making me feel alive, and I smell this strange water but it's familiar in some way, like one of them strange *I been here before* feelings.

Things comes down to matters of timing. That's what Callie would say. Don't miss your chance when it comes around. Brandi too, she'd say the same. She'll have gone through the house by now. She's found the note and spitefully commenced to cuss me. She probably ransacked all the drawers, knowing it ain't gonna do no good, yet she done it anyhow, screeching like a goose in heat. I can't stand it when she gets like that.

And then Prescott, that sleazy mudcat, done got his mug on the front page of the paper in a way he surely ain't proud of. Why'd I ever wanna give five thousand dollars of my money to a scum like that? Even if he did bury Callie. Who'd of ever thought it, that he'd a gone and got hisself mixed up with such folks? And him wanting to question *my* honor. Good thing he's got Mr. T. Stanley Bueron to look out after him. May justice be done by you, Mr. Prescott.

The boat turns a little and the light's out of my eyes now. The water's moving fast and the wind's in my hair, trailing it behind me. I'm looking down and she comes in view and I'm looking at her in the waves and she's all there, no empty spaces—like that last piece of puzzle done been found.

When I look up, I see her in full view and she's taller than I ever thought, raising her torch and standing there sure as eternity itself, glimmering green in the sun, and I have to say it's a sight like I never seen before. All a matter of timing, it is. I reach down and feel in my pocket. I know it's still there, yet it don't hurt to be extra careful. I touch it, all rolled up with a rubber band, safe and sound and plenty of it left. I'm looking at them rays coming out of her head, seven of em. One for each sea, they told us back on shore. Or was it one for each continent? A big world, it is. Lots of it to see and I ain't yet got started good. I roll the rubber band with my thumb and think about that St. Louis Arch and that Golden Gate Bridge. She's towering above me now, making me feel like a little speck, and the boat's pulling up to the dock. It ain't even noon yet, and there's so much more to go.

## Make Me an Angel

There was no more milk in the apartment so she knew the crying would go on. And it did. Until she could no longer bear it and so fixed his twice-weaned mouth against her nipple and closed her eyes. Across the room, the radiator clanged like a maniacal kettledrum. Below, an ambulance's siren. At last, she felt the outflow of her milk and laid her head back against the couch.

Her lawyer didn't lend out money, he reminded her again. But he understood, he assured her that he understood. Wasn't he doing all he could? Was it his fault the worker's compensation insurance carrier had gone bankrupt? At least she'd gotten the operation first. And it wasn't just *her* check that had stopped, you see, but everyone else's too. Nothing to worry about, though—the state maintained a guaranty fund. Payments should resume soon. In the meantime—couldn't she stop that baby from crying—in the meantime, weren't there relief agencies? Charities? Something like that?

She lay under a quilt on the couch, her back flat against the cushions, knees pulled to her chest. The radiator was quiet. The radio was on in the kitchen. Bonnie Raitt. The apartment was very cold. *Just give me one thing . . . that I can hold onto.* When the crying began, she threw off the quilt and rolled to the floor on all fours, used the armrest to gain her feet. She went first to the bathroom, opened the container of Demerol and looked at the one pill rolling heedlessly around the bottom. The crying swelled. She closed the bottle and put it away, the pill still inside. Then she warmed the last of the milk she had bought with the charity money and made a bottle.

Later, she counted what was left of the money, figured, pocketed the bills in her coat. The baby slept. She went out of the apartment and put her key in the deadbolt and set her forehead square against the door with her eyes shut. The drugstore was three blocks away. She crossed herself in the way she had seen Catholics do. Then she turned the key.

She stopped twice during the first two blocks to lean her back against whatever building or wall there was, only stopped once during the third block.

Inside the drugstore, it was warm. She looked at the shelves of formula, figured some more, put a few cans in her basket, figured again, put a can back. She watched the clerk's eyes as she came down the aisle of cold and pain remedies. Glued to her. She stopped before the rows of aspirin and ibuprofen. Another customer entered and the clerk looked away. Just for a second.

At the counter, she reached into her pocket for the bills and felt the ibuprofen package, thought she heard the pills rattling loudly, felt the accusatorial eye of the clerk undressing her down to her burgeoning heartbeat. She gave the clerk the bills and took the change and put the coins in the opposite pocket, didn't count it, didn't stop walking until she was half a block from the apartment building. Leaning back against a wall, she opened the ibuprofen box and threw the box to the sidewalk and watched the wind take it down the night. She tore away the seal and poured out four of the pills, swallowed them two at a time. One more alley to cross. One more alley, and that was where she saw the movement.

The boy pulled her in and shoved her hard against the wall, his hand over her mouth. His skin was coarse and vile tasting. She saw the switchblade click before her eyes, and behind the glint of steel, a scared and purulent mask of depravity. A missing front tooth. He took her sack and flung away the cans of formula and they trundled down the alley drunkenly. Then into her pockets, took the few coins, slung the ibuprofen bottle against the pavement. The top came unfastened and pills rolled about bewilderedly like knob-cornered dice. When he left, she dropped to her knees. The asphalt smelled of rancid sauerkraut. She gathered up the cans and what of the pills she could find. Wind tunneled through the alley like the repercussions of a ghostly freight-train and the wind was very cold. In the distance, a lone cry, perhaps that of a small child. She rose and stumbled toward her building, entered and pulled herself up the stairs. Later, she took the last Demerol.

She lay on the couch all of the next day, except when she got up to feed the baby or change a diaper or relieve her bladder. The following morning, she rose and tidied up the kitchen. She sat down at the kitchen table with a pencil and paper, wrote down the amount of her rent, did some figuring, then lay down on the couch again.

That afternoon, she gathered up the four Limoges boxes that had been her grandmother's and carefully wrapped them in old newspaper and put them in a small sack. She took her baby and the sack and walked thirty minutes and five blocks to a pawn shop where she unwrapped the boxes and spread them across the counter. The proprietor studied them. He told her ten dollars apiece. She said they were worth a hundred each. He gave her fifty for them all. She put the ticket in her pocket and walked to the bus stop.

Her lawyer told her not to come again without an appointment. And not to bring the baby. Not ever to bring the baby again. Didn't she understand he was doing all he could? The payments would resume soon. The state was involved and bureaucrats moved slowly. These things took time. She sat and listened and when he was quiet, she continued to sit. The lawyer watched her through the precipitous silence. A taxidermied raccoon stared down from the bookcase, subtle bemusement encased within its glass eye. From behind, a clock ticked. The lawyer watched her still. He took out his wallet and removed two twenties, slid them across the desk. But she must understand that this was all. And that she couldn't tell anyone else because, after all, he couldn't afford to lend money to all of his clients, now, could he?

At the grocery, she bought a half gallon of milk, four

apples, a loaf of white bread, a dozen jars of baby food, and three cans of tuna. When she got home, the notice was tacked to her door. She tore it off and took it inside. It said that she had ten days to pay the rent. Or move. She fixed a bottle for the baby, ate a can of the tuna and a little of the white bread. Then she took four of the ibuprofen and lay down on the couch. On the radio was a song she didn't recognize.

She sat across the desk from the housing project manager, a gray-haired matron with a dour face who asked her questions and wrote down her answers on a form. The manager punched numbers into a calculator, told her how much the rent would be, told her what it would go to when . . . if . . . her comp payments resumed. But they were full now anyway, though something might come available next month. She would put her on the waiting list. She should check back in two weeks.

When she left the office, it was near-dark. She walked through the cold, carrying the child. She looked for a bus stop, but the streets were unfamiliar to her. They were desolate streets, wind-scarred and potholed, converging at obtuse and asymmetrical angles, and she could fix upon no point of reference. Craggy buildings loomed helter-skelter all about her, grotesque and threatening structures that listed arthritically, like gnarled dilapidations conceived in the belladonna dreams of a mad architect. She wandered lost through the derangement and night soon overtook her. In an alley mouth, she came upon a bearded man in a white robe. The robe was marred with splotches of darkness. In one hand he held a trident, in the other, a giant conch shell. He smelled of alcohol and urine. He declared to her that Calypso had betrayed him and that he would have his vengeance. She walked on.

The wind blew through her coat and clothing, shook her body in frigid, perfervid spasms. The baby cried louder. Presently, she came to an unlit alley and looked down it to where an orange fire burned in a metal drum. Nondescript people huddled about like wraiths. She approached, held one hand to the fire, clutched her baby tighter with the other.

The smoke was infused with a putrid, burnt-meat smell, and it made her eyes water.

Across the barrel was a man in a dark cloak. He slipped his hood back to reveal a shard of his face in the firelight. His flesh was misshapen with lesions. He asked her what was the child's name. She didn't answer. His eyes glimmered satanically. He asked again, louder this time. What was the child's name? She backed away. He said that he liked children and then he smiled. He was missing a front tooth.

She lurched toward the mouth of the alley, choruses of laughter echoing behind her. On the street, a car raced toward her. She flagged at it as it sped by.

She wandered aimlessly. Block after block through the depraved streets with the gaining wind and the gauzy streetlights. Before her there suddenly appeared a flume of vapor swirling upward from a sidewalk grate. She went to the grate and sat down on it and the rising steam cocooned her in a fog of warmth. She sat there cross-legged with the child to her chest, head bowed toward the netherworld below. For a long time she sat in that way, her eyes shut against the night. When she looked up, the hulking silhouette of a human figure towered above her. Steam rose behind the vague form, diffusing the streetlight into a steely, monochromatic aureole. A man's voice spoke, told her he was there to help her. She sat wordlessly, looking up into the light.

She had bathed and put on cologne and a white terry-cloth robe and was waiting in her apartment when the knock came. She approached the door and paused. The baby was sleeping and the apartment was very quiet. She stood, looked at the door, and waited for the knock to come a second time. When it did, she cleared her throat silently and crossed herself.

The man was dressed pleasantly in woolen slacks and a skier's sweater. He looked at her nervously. She smiled and invited him in. He moved cautiously into the room, looking around as if he expected something to spring upon him from a corner. He removed some bills from his wallet and handed them to her. From the hall came voices, Spanish accents in broken English. She undid the sash and opened her robe outward as if unfurling wings. She thought she heard a girl's voice singing. She tried to recognize the song.

## Sailing into Orion

I am thankful for small blessings: slow-moving afternoons, Millie bringing green tea, the turning leaves of the red maple, the gray smell of November rain. She has spent the morning laboring over the house, has Millie, meticulously dusting and waxing, even polishing the silver—what there is left of it after two divorces—wanting things to be perfect for Suzannah. Her time is a commodity, purchasable with my dollars. Still enough of those, thank goodness. Her time I can buy, but my own hours are beyond the reach of commerce. A less than subtle irony at the bottom of that, but I am no longer amused by irony.

Time, I have discovered, is both a blessing and a curse to the dying—each second precious in its own right, yet reach out for it and time slides ahead and the moment vanishes, the thread unspooling its way toward the end and no way to rewind it. Thornhill's Paradox, I call it. Why not claim the credit for myself? It adds a breath of permanence to the temporal, to me, to that vague collection of memories bound to drift through the consciousness of my remaining friends like ghostly jellyfish in the watery light of an aquarium. My own private space in the cosmos of thought.

Millie, bless her meddlesome heart, has made this day complete—invited her brother, Brother Darwin Steptoe, to drop in for an early evening visit. She means well, so I don't complain, just wince a bit. Give her the smooth outer edge of my rough inner revulsion. If she were not so good to me, I would expose my sardonic soul with an eruption that would leave her in tears. But where's the fun in that? I'll tolerate Brother Darwin for one last visit. Then, I'll talk to her honestly, tell her I don't bear well his phony evangelical smile and his manicured voice betraying every tenet of English grammar as he tries so fervently to usher my incorrigible soul toward Paradise. His visits are all the same, and I have no time for repetitious things. He'll open with some pathetic joke, probably to do with money or vice, then he'll launch into one of his painful war stories. Finally, we'll "have prayer," as if prayer were a consumable I might order out for and have Millie carve up like pizza so that we can all partake. "Would you care for another slice of prayer, Brother Darwin? And you, Millie? You look like you could use a bit more yourself." But tonight I'll humor them. Maybe even request a little divine intervention for Suzannah's visit. What could it hurt?

It's funny, the disparate memories that lodge in the folds of the brain, that stick there so firmly that time can't shake them loose. Like that part of *Peter Pan* where Peter tells Wendy the way to Neverland. Second star to the right and straight on till morning. It was Suzannah's favorite story, back when her childhood imagination was on the cusp of surrender and she was caught in that doubtful space between myth and truth, not quite ready to let go of things and places that live only in the mind. I remember those clear wintry nights on the back deck where we would watch Orion rising above the trees and I would name off the stars for her: Betelgeuse, the red giant with its rusted-orange hue; Rigel, brilliant as a diamond; Bellatrix, the hunter's western shoulder; then the string of pearls, Mintaka, Alnilam and Alnitak, the three stars of the belt. "There it is," I would say, pointing to Alnilam, "the second star," and we would set our eyes against our celestial road sign, the two of us wrapped in our coats and our singular dream, turning our minds right at that star and gliding effortlessly toward morning. Life was a downhill slide then, pirates breathing at our backs, fairies our guardians, curiosity our sovereign. Never in the vastness of that universe opening above us could I have imagined how we would unravel, how circumstances would bring us to estrangement.

Yet here I lie, time running away from me like water through splayed fingers, and I have not seen my daughter in over fifteen years.

Millie is comfort exalted, but her familiarity works against me. My guard slips and she sees my every nervous insecurity. She doesn't let on, but I can tell what she's feeling and it's far too close to pity. A damnable emotion and one I cannot abide when I am its object.

"It's all going to be fine," she assures me. "She wants this as much as you."

"You think you know her mind, do you?"

"I have a feel for these things."

"You have a need to tack happy endings onto every story."

"I'm right about this," she reassures. "You'll see."

"I'm dying to find out," I deadpan. She backs away, smiling awkwardly, uncertainly, then goes off in search of some new chore to tackle.

The rain stops and I make my daily pilgrimage to the backyard, carefully wrapped by Millie in a wool sweater that's too heavy for the temperature. Mattson, my octogenarian neighbor, is cutting up a dead sourwood with his chainsaw, piling the logs where our fences corner. He is thin and jaunty, always smiling. He shuts down the saw and waves to me as I totter down the three steps, Millie at my arm. I ought to get a cane, but I abhor the thought of it and I have a right to act irrationally at this point. "Afternoon, Thornhill," he shouts in his New England accent, a remnant of his past that he never lost, though he has lived in the south for better than twenty years. "Good to see you out."

"You're gonna strain your feeble old back," I warn as he makes ready to lift a sizeable log.

"Weatherman says frost in the morning. Cold front coming down, don't you know." He picks up the log, heaves it onto the pile and brushes his hands down the front of his Boston College sweatshirt, eagle mascot and all, then throws his chest out like a puckish egret. "Big game tomorrow, Thornhill."

"My bookie says take the Irish, lay the points."

"Bad advice," he chides. "Best to take the points and lay the Irish. I did that once. A buxom red-haired lass from Killarney." His eyes arc with ancient mischief.

I make a brief trek around my grounds, then take my accustomed seat in the lawnchair. The nausea is not so bad this afternoon so I linger, watching Mattson piddle about, revving his chainsaw and stacking his limbs. Finally, the cold begins seeping through my sweater.

"Come around tomorrow before the game," I shout over the chainsaw as I head back toward the house. "Millie'll make us tea. Maybe make you something stronger."

He waves to me, face all asmile, then drops the saw into the downed tree trunk and carves off another log.

Later, the nausea returns, so my supper is scant. A small bowl of oatmeal, slices of some unidentifiable fruit that Millie has cut up. I eat slowly and retire to my couch, just in time for the dreaded arrival of Brother Darwin. Millie shows the scalawag in.

"You're looking good, Brother Thornhill," he lies.

"How's Mama?" I ask. If I've got to be his brother, aren't I entitled to know?

"Mama?" He's slow at grasping sarcasm, but several seconds of probing my caustic expression and he's right there with me, laughing too loud, grinning like he's just hauled up a collection plate overspilling with twenties. "Oh, *Mama*. Mama's fine. Just got out of prison and been celebrating all day with white lightning. She's all the time asking about you."

"Glad to hear it," I say, as he nests himself into my leather recliner, shifting his heft about to fix upon the most comfortable position. "I like being made a fuss over."

"What can I have Millie get you?" he asks cheerfully, his face flushed in a cherry, high-blood-pressure patina. He reeks of cheap men's cologne.

"Glenlivet. Neat."

"Got that Millie? One neat Glen-whatchamacallit."

Millie rolls back her eyes, feigning disgust. "I'll get you

a Coke, Darwin," she says, scurrying off to the kitchen. "And apple juice for you, Mr. Thornhill."

Brother Darwin leans in, gearing up for one of his serious how-to-face-death-like-a-Christian monologs. I am too weak for confrontation, so I follow the course of least resistance. Meaning I lie there and listen, hoping he'll soon tire. I am, I tell myself, paying for my old sins. At least I will die debt-free.

Old sins. They have their own way of warping through time to coat the present with their stain. Leslie was a line I couldn't wait to cross, knew I would cross from the moment she first appeared at the office, knit sweater and plaid skirt hugging her every curve and camber, glassy-black hair swooping about like van Gogh brushstrokes. I was forty-three then, she twenty-one, only four years older than Suzannah. I knew the world would change forever, that the deck of all life's chances was about to be reshuffled with no guarantees of where the important cards would land. I never pled confusion, never blamed that tired old need for greater space. Leslie was a well-chosen sin, our actions, expressions of our own free and faulty wills. And so it went. A year, a couple of months, then the inevitable exposure. We carried on through the bitter fallout, married each other shortly after the divorce. We were trying, I suppose, to encircle the passion that we both must have realized was bleeding away too rapidly. Needless to say, we failed.

Brother Darwin sips his Coke, drones on. We speak of other places and times. New Orleans comes up. He was there once, saving souls at Jackson Square with an evangelist from Knoxville name of Tom Paul Courtney. "A burly, fearless man of God," Brother Darwin describes him. "Piloted Hueys in "Nam. Come face to face with his maker more times than Clinton lied. But God was riding in that helicopter with him."

"Probably right next to the gunner," I surmise.

"Anyway, we spy out these two harlots, spike heels, purple fingernails, fishnet stockings, the whole shootin' match. We walk up to 'em and one of 'em rubs a hand down Tom

Paul's arm, calls him Hansom Boy and wants to know what does he do for a living. 'Me and my partner here work for the Big Man,' he says. 'And we're looking for a little action.' So they invite us to come along, but Tom Paul gets in the lead and we're all following him. He scoots through a little side door and Glory, the next thing you know we're standing in the kitchen of some restaurant, and them harlots are looking at one another like what in creation's going on. Well, Tom Paul, he walks right over to where this cook's grilling crawfish cakes. He takes them harlots' wrists, one in each hand, and wham, before they know what's happened, he's slammed their hands palm-down on top of that grill. Picked 'em up right quick so's they didn't burn too bad, but Glory, what screaming and cussing did come forth from 'em. Then Brother Tom Paul commenced to preaching. Told 'em how he just give 'em a tiny taste of what hell's gonna be like. That hell's gonna burn 'em head to toe and much hotter than that little grill because hell's the Devil's own fire, hotter by a long shot than anything man ever come up against. Glory, did them harlots' faces go pale. They turned and run like panicked chipmunks. Time the head cook had run us out, they was long gone. But I tell you, Brother Thornhill, I tell you and I believe it to this day, that revelation turned 'em in a new and glorious direction. Yes sir, Brother Tom Paul saved them two souls from eternal damnation."

Mercifully, Millie enters, says it's time for her to leave and that maybe Brother Darwin ought to think about wrapping up his visit. Amazing grace, how sweet the sound.

"Let's have prayer," says Brother Darwin.

"Just a small piece for me," I say. He gives me a hesitant look, then smiles and takes my hand while he serves up a rousing plea that God's will be done. He leaves, promising more prayers and another visit. Right. The Vatican will underwrite abortion clinics before this drunk-on-Jesus cowboy wipes his boots on my doormat again. But I will address this with Millie tomorrow. For now, I'm satisfied just to be left alone in my own house. Praise the Lord.

I married Joan a year out of college. Two years later,

we had Suzannah. Named her after Joan's grandmother. I've always loved the sonorous resonance of the name, a profound and earnest name, so unlike the flippant-sounding *Joan*. We had our early stage of passion, Joan and I, seemed well-suited to each other, made great love and great family pictures, the pictures always featuring Suzannah arranged between us, always beaming joy. We displayed the outward signs of a happy family, but passion, like a storm, cannot sustain, and when it expends itself, it leaves a hungry vacuum. We could never seem to replenish the emptiness, so we drifted along on marital cruise-control, a cardboard relationship requiring little effort, yielding less reward. Were it not for Suzannah, our marriage would have disintegrated sooner, possibly with a more honorable resolution, surely with less pain. But ultimately, even Suzannah could not resurrect what had already died. Did I think our failed relationship excused infidelity? I don't think I looked at it that way. I don't think I thought about it at all. Leslie was there, we wanted each other, there seemed nothing of importance at risk, things came together. Only later would I realize my miscalculation.

My memory has evolved into a treacherous bitch, spilling away useful knowledge at an astonishing rate, yet not letting go of those poisonous images that randomly torment me: Joan thrusting the investigator's pictures at me, hysterical, demanding that I leave, Suzannah refusing my farewell embrace, Suzannah standing in the door, eyes blood-rimmed, her face imploding, her lips mouthing the word *how*. Over and over, that word *how*, me hearing it with my eyes and then with my memory, but not answering because it wasn't really a question, hearing it echo as I drove away, *how*, not understanding even then that my past had been severed, that the ground I stood on had sheared away and left me alone looking back across an ever-widening gulf, and Suzannah on the opposite shore fading from sight, her question that wasn't a question ricocheting through me, *how*, ricocheting through the burgeoning abyss between us, *how, how, how*.

I struggle to my feet, clamber to the back door. Walking is no longer a thoughtless shuffling of feet. This menace eating me from the inside-out requires that I devote an unnatural measure of awareness to the procedure. One foot ahead, secure balance, lift back foot, position it forward of the other, secure balance again. A tiresome way to travel, but I am in no hurry.

A steely chill has seeped into the early evening, more than my sweater will long hold at bay. I search the sky for my hunter friend, but it is too early, he has not risen, so I settle into my lawnchair. The neighborhood is quiet, the cold not yet unbearable. The lights from Mattson's windows are yellow and warm. I could sleep here, at home under these stars, let the cold take me when it will. There are worse exits. An intense and profound serenity overcomes me, an assurance that the night is closing in, covering me with its strange and ageless comforts, its myths and mysteries. Each moment I remain makes my rising less probable. If this earth could turn faster, could spin Orion above these treetops. Or bring me into tomorrow, to Suzannah and this time I have asked for, this appointment I must keep.

The cold hits me hard, takes advantage of my weakness. I fight my way through the daze like a diver struggling to the surface, take my gasp of air and begin moving toward the house. Time I reach the door, I'm rocked in shivers, can barely make my bedroom. Two quilts and an electric blanket and I submerge myself into a jerking fetal position, holding on against the spasms that roll through me. Too weak to even turn out the lights. Probably I'll wake up later in a sweat.

Suzannah's flight has been delayed, Millie reports as she hangs up the phone. Not expected in until three o'clock. Waiting should be anathema to one in my skin, yet I seem to need the time. I need to imagine our reunion, how it will unfold, what touchings and tears will be exchanged, the forgiveness that will be granted me. But I know about wishful thinking, understand risk-taking. It's a delicate balance, this equation I'm trying to solve. The fulcrum could shift, plans could veer off course. I knew that when I resolved to make the call. Maybe I should have let sleeping dogs lie, but I was bolstered by the courage of one with nothing to lose. And I had old memories in need of massaging, in need of a real voice for me to hear and real flesh for me to touch and real eyes to look into when I seek my absolution.

One of the daughters answered—Melinda, the ten-year-old, if I had to guess. They know only one grandfather, the two girls, so no need to confuse issues. All she knew was that a Mr. Thornhill called for Mom. It will be Suzannah's prerogative to explain me. Or not. It went about as I had expected—first the surprise, maybe you could say shock. Then a cold tone, noncommittal, matter-of-fact. I was not dissuaded. I didn't beg, just asked. The difference is important. She spoke between long pauses, gave me tentative words, hesitant phrasings, finally a provisional commitment. The status quo had been pierced, but what next? What happens when we face each other? Maybe she'll lock eyes and tell me nothing's changed, that hell's the one place left for me to traipse off to. Fine, then. I won't have long to fret over it anyway. No harm, no foul, nothing to lose.

A pattern has emerged, the sickness worsening with the afternoon. And the pain. I have my ace-in-the-hole liquid morphine, but I have avoided it today in lieu of a clearer mind. Meanwhile, Millie bumps about like a pinball, constantly repositioning table whatnots as if I had sadistically rearranged them while her back was turned. Her bothersome energy annoys me.

"Can I fix you tea?" she wants to know.

"Can you not just settle down?" I ask.

"I just want things to be right."

"God forbid that glass bowl should be a quarter-inch off center. She'll probably turn around and walk right out."

"Everything has its proper place, Mr. Thornhill."

"Fix the tea. Fix you a cup too and come sit down a minute. Before you drive out the last remnant of my sanity."

She returns with two cups, strong and bitter, the way I've always taken it. It does not much agree with my illness, but this is no time to begin amending customs.

"What do you suppose got into me?" I ask. "Calling her after all this time?"

"You wanted to see her. Wanted to know about her life. To make your peace."

"Do you think that was it? Or is it the other way around? Is it that I want *her* to know about *my* life?"

"Maybe a little of both."

"I think it's more the latter. That I want her to know me. Who I was. To have some grain of regard for who I was."

"That's natural."

"Or selfish. I think it's selfish."

"It's not selfish at all. It was a brave thing for you to call her."

"It's brave of her to come. She's got her own life, her own family. Why would she want to take on the added baggage of watching me die?"

"Oh, Mr. Thornhill. Don't say that."

"Maybe she's afraid I'd cut her out of the will."

"No. Stop it, now."

"Or maybe it's morbid curiosity. Seeing me get what I've deserved after all these years."

"Stop it, I said."

"Rotting away like a swamp log, and she wants a look. A firsthand view of divine justice bludgeoning me to dust."

She stands, her eyes gathering moisture. "I'm not going to listen to this. I'm just not."

"I pay you to listen to me, remember?"

"No sir. No you do not pay me to listen to . . . to *that*." She walks into the kitchen.

"Bring me some goddamn morphine, then," I shout after her. "I'm sure I pay you to do that."

"No. I won't do it." The teary weakness in her voice annoys me. "She'll be here soon. You can wait."

"What are you crying about anyway? It's me that's dying here, remember?"

She does not answer. I can hear her infuriating sobs from the kitchen. Goddamn the world. I lay back on the couch, close my eyes and watch the darkness spin. Now I feel remorse. What a useless human emotion, remorse. Always coming too late to save us from our wickedness. Never arriving in time to prevent our missteps. Goddamn the world. Goddamn the whole shit-laden world.

Four-fifteen. I wash my face for the fourth time, try to arrange my thinning hair and garbled clothing into a less frightening appearance. I have made my peace with the ever-forgiving Millie. If I make it until Christmas, I must do something extra nice for her.

As the minutes tick by, we are both thinking the same thing, that maybe she's reneged, that the burden of this reunion has proven too extreme and that she has turned the rental car around and headed back to the airport to catch the next plane home. We do not speak of such a possibility, but it is a simple matter for me to trespass on Millie's thoughts. I believe it would affect her more than me. I have come to terms with this. I could not blame Suzannah for standing me up, will not blame her if that is indeed what has occurred. Whatever happens, I am at peace with it.

It is near to four-thirty when the doorbell rings. Millie's gaze meets mine for a bare instant, then she is off to get the door. I get to my feet and am standing when they enter. She looks . . . not exactly as I had expected—the cherubic curves of her girl's cheeks have succumbed to early middle age, but I can recall where they went, can trace with my memory how they once lay against her face and skin. There is a sad and nervous appearance in her eyes and she approaches me as though perhaps I might bite. The moment is awkward, though more so for her, I'm sure. I hold out my arm like a giant wing and she walks into my embrace. Millie, my favorite Millie, is smiling as if one of us, it wouldn't matter who, had just won the lottery. I give her a gusty wink.

I offer Suzannah wine, but she decides on tea. Millie brings us steaming cups, then disappears. She is, no doubt, sitting quietly in the kitchen, just out of sight, ear cocked in the direction of our voices.

"What a long time it's been," I start out, unable to come up with anything better.

"It has. I'm glad you called."

"I talk to your mother once a year or so. She tells me you got promoted. That you're a vice-president now."

She gives me a retreating smile. "It's more form than substance, I'm afraid. But yes, it's nice to get the recognition."

"And Perry? He's doing well?"

"He started his own consulting business last year. I guess she told you that. It's going well. We're pleased."

"And the girls. Melinda and Regan. Ten and seven?"

"Ten and eight. Going on sixteen and twenty-one." She laughs.

"My God." I sip the tea, my eyes on her. "How did I ever let you get so far away from me?"

She looks at the floor, then back to me. "I guess that's what I'm here to find out."

"Your mom, she never let go of it. All the anger and the hurt. I can understand that, I guess. But with you it was different. I thought time would have brought you back to me before now."

She stirs her tea thoughtfully, balances her spoon on the saucer. "Betrayal was something that happened in other families. It wasn't supposed to happen in ours."

"Betrayal. That's a nasty, unforgiving word."

"Is there a better word for it?"

"Words are nothing but symbols. Inadequate symbols, in most cases. Like the word rejection. Inadequate to describe these last fifteen years."

"What did you expect?" Her eyes are within my own, her adult eyes that I can no longer read with the confidence of the past.

"Some small measure of understanding. Eventual forgiveness. Some attempt at reconciliation."

"I can forgive you. I'm not that cruel-hearted."

"I never believed you were cruel-hearted."

"It's just that when you married her . . . my God, Daddy. Where was I supposed to fit into that?"

"It's not unheard of to have a tolerable relationship with a stepparent."

"Oh, come on. She was practically *my* age."

Her eyes water. There are no good replies to her argument. I sip the tea, hold her gaze while the hostility settles. "So, are you happy? With Perry? With your job? With your life?"

She smiles at the window. "Big questions."

"My turn to ask questions now."

"I guess that's fair then. Yeah, my life is good. Perry's a wonderful husband. My work is satisfying. And the girls . . . ." She smiles, fingertips a cord of her blond hair behind an ear. "Yeah, I'd have to say my life is good."

"You read to them a lot?"

"All the time. But you'd know that, wouldn't you?"

"I had a hunch."

"Like father, like daughter, huh?"

Her hands fall lightly into her lap, the diamond catching the afternoon light, focusing it into a single peak of brilliance. I want to reach out for that hand, to hold onto that hand and to this unstable peace teetering between us. But the time is not right, and I know I have to risk disrupting this moment, have to go that final step and open the last door where I know more pain is lurking, but there is something there I have to discover. "Look, Suzannah, I'm in no position to be judgmental. So don't take this in that way. But . . . there were eighteen years there between us." I look into her eyes, her adult eyes that I can no longer plumb to their foundation. "What happened to those years? Where did that time go that you couldn't bring yourself to call me? I just need to know that, because I—"

"You haven't tried to contact me either. You haven't written in years. The phone dials from either end. The mail runs both ways."

"I called and wrote regularly for four years. Have you forgotten?"

She swallows, takes a labored breath. "No." She looks out the window to where the wind ripples the maple's crimson leaves. "And I should have answered. But during those first years, I was too . . . too . . . ." Her voice cracks, trails off into a headshake.

"I never meant for the pain to land so hard on you."

"I'm sorry," she says, reaching for a tissue. "Of course

you didn't really know what I was going through then. After I came out on the other side of it, things were different. I met Perry, we had Melinda, my life was suddenly full, overflowing. It seemed like there wasn't room enough to let the past back in. So I didn't call you. Though I did think about you. Many times, I thought about calling. But I always put it off. Something to do tomorrow."

A cant of butterscotch light streaks across her face. This image of her, sitting contemplatively, hands folded in her lap, is one I want to keep. "It doesn't matter," I say. "You're here now. Just talk to me about yourself, your family. Show me pictures of the girls."

She reaches out for me and I sit up. We embrace, holding on as if we are reaching out an empty bucket, a bucket fifteen years deep, holding it at the wellhead and waiting for it to fill. When she pulls away, her eyes are wet. She laughs and reaches for the tissue box, hands me one too. "How did you know I'd bring pictures?" she asks.

We talk on into the evening. Millie fixes us sandwiches, joins us for a bite. She asks about my disease, the medications and the pain, how much time there is left. But I dispense with this topic quickly. I am practiced at tactfully redirecting conversation away from my morbid secrets. Otherwise, the talk is of her, of Melinda and Regan. And there is laughter, the mirth-filled voice that has not sounded against my ear in more than fifteen years filling me with comfort—I could almost say hope. She has reserved a room at a local motel, but decides instead to stay in my guest bedroom. She must fly back tomorrow, but will return soon, before Christmas for sure, she says. Maybe even bring Melinda and Regan, depending upon . . . circumstances.

Long after Millie's departure, we walk, at my insistence, in the backyard. The night is cold, but Suzannah has bundled me like a mummy, so the discomfort is tolerable. As we walk, an explosion of darkness seizes us, as if the night has claimed some sudden and profound dominion over the ground where we stand, exiling any rumor of ambient light. She looks at me, puzzled. "Power failure," I explain. "Damn power company can't keep the squirrels out of their transformers. It shouldn't be out long."

The purity of the night is startling, assailing me with self-awareness. Sheets of newborn stars emerge above us, shy stars, disdainful of competing with manmade light, winking down on us now by sheer chance from unreckonable distances, revealing pieces of night that go unseen, except by eyes that purposely seek out this extreme and relentless darkness. She looks up into the inviolable depths, up to where the Milky Way's ancient arm crests above us like the vanishing spoor of a prehistoric race of celestial nomads. Like me, she is a stargazer, possessing that singular quality of heart capable of absorbing times and places only the imagination can touch. It pleases me in a strange way, this image of her staring at the heavens. I start to mention it, but swallow my words. Instead, I leave her suspended in her own moment of fragile amazement and turn my gaze to the east where my old friend Orion is rising above the trees. And I wonder about my grandchildren, wonder about their connection to these stars and the stories she has told them, wonder whether some infinitesimal part of me has been passed along in the telling.

Soon, the cold drives us inside. By the time we have sought out and lit the candles, the power is back, returning with the same abruptness with which it left. She offers to make more tea, but I decline. I am spent, and sleep offers the greater peace for me now. She unwraps the layers of clothing, helps me to my bedroom, tells me goodnight, kisses me on the cheek, says she might open that bottle of Chardonnay in the refrigerator. The corkscrew, I tell her, is in the drawer to the left of the sink.

In the dark, I lie on my back beneath the sheets and the sky opens above me. I feel her presence near to me, no more than my wishful thoughts I know, but it does not matter now—these borders between imagination and reality have become kindly porous and unguarded. We are flying now, the two of us, the great hunter above, the pearly stars of his belt beckoning like a muezzin's chant, and we are coursing toward a place we have been before, a long age ago, a place where time arrests itself and change is illusion, gliding along at the speed of dreams, finding our marker, turning right at the second star and sailing on toward morning.

# Sabbath

Stinging cold then. Always it starts with the cold. Then the day remembers itself and I am powerless—a leaf upon the rapids. Stinging icewater air and frosted morning-ground crunching beneath the soles of manboots and the flint February dawn there in the room with me, the heaviness of the quilts pressing me warm and I remember wanting not to move—wanting to lie there cocooned in old bed linen with smells of woodsmoke and Mamma frying bacon like every Sunday.

*"Git up, Stell. You gone make us late for church."*

*And then the sound of firelogs breaking and I look out. The hearth is alive and warm because Sam Junior's standing there with a steel poker like he's stabbing at a dragon and the dragon's spitting out fire and Mamma's at the stove, turning bacon and her voice coming to me like in a song.*

*"Don't want me to tell Pastor Briarwood you done gone and made us late again now do you?"*

*Now I'm on the floor standing and Boss is moving under me—his black coat sliding along up under and his tail moving, hitting up against the bottoms of the floorboards—and my bare feet feel the winter in the floor and the wind between the cracks.*

*"Git ya socks on, girl. You gone take the pneumonia in them bare feet."*

*I get them on and hurry to the hearth and the popping fire. Heat is pouring warm off the logs and I hold my hands out flat to the rising heat and the fire makes me warm all through. The room is full with bacon frying because it's Sunday and the smell makes me hungry.*

We lived no more than a quarter mile from the Catawba River. The white folks called it "under the hill" because it lay beneath a soaring red-clay bluff, under the town of Conrad, Alabama. Spring rains often swelled the Catawba out of its banks until we could see the rising muddy water from our porch and the smell of the river would wander through the house like a welcomed guest and we would watch the water as it crept through the bald cypress trees across the road in a flat, rusty plain. "You stay off from that water," Mamma would order us. "Moccasins'll be out crawling. They gone be hungry for little chillun." But Sam Junior would go right out in the river anyway, taking out with Mose Jackson in his granddaddy's old johnboat, and I'd walk out on the big rocks where the water came at its high point and dip my hands in the river and we were never bothered by any moccasins, though I did always keep a sharp lookout.

One year, the water got high as Miz Eula Thompson's back porch and that's when the old folks started talking about how in nineteen-o-something-or-other, the river rose halfway up the bluff and all of under the hill was under water and there was even a railroad tie jammed in the top of a big chinaberry tree halfway up the bluff, which proved how high the water had come.

In the winter, the west wind would climb off the river raw and cold and push up against the bluff and when the wind was strong and angry, it would whistle through the cracks and crevices of our house and rattle the boards and the tin sheets of the roof and ride up against the bluff moaning like a song until it poured over the crest of the hill and pushed on through to Conrad and across the flatlands beyond the town and on toward Georgia. Then spring would come, and the discomforts of those bitter winds would turn like pages into reassuring warmth as the earth resurrected itself, and the steep clay bank covered over with green shrubs and wild blackberries with briers that stuck cruel and deep whenever you climbed up through them. At the top was Jackdaw Street, where the poorest of the white folks lived. Looking out east, you could see across the flat cotton fields and on beyond to where the wind went when it left Conrad. It was a secret, hallowed place, spilling over with desire—full of thirst for what lay beyond immediate reach. Pastor Briarwood used to talk about the ocean, about how you could stand in the sand and look out to sea and there was nothing but water as far as you could see and how the sky and water became one seamless space where you could feel the presence of the Almighty in every gust of wind. In the fall, when the cotton fields were bursting in white and waving in the river breezes, I often thought about the ocean and whether it could possibly be as endless as those fields and if it looked anything like those waves of cotton as they rolled easy under the wind.

* * *

Dr. St. James motions me into the hall, his green surgical suit contrasting absurdly with the stark and sterile whiteness of the hospital. His smile is forced—it says, *abandon all hope,* though he does not mean for it to be read so. He is kind. His words come as softly as the weight of his hand on my shoulder or the tears that well in my eyes. He is sending William to Dr. Milligan, a pediatric oncologist. The best, he assures me. There is a new chemotherapy available. There is good cause for hope. We must not lose hope.

* * *

*Mama sets a plate of biscuits on the table and a glass of milk for me. My socks are thick and hold the heat from the fire while I sit at the table. Sam Junior's going at the bacon like a whirlwind and Mamma has to tell him to slow down so we can all get some. The bacon's warm and salty and tastes as good as it smells. Mamma's telling us a story like on every Sunday. Three men being thrown into a fiery furnace and they have funny sounding names that I can't remember at first but she keeps repeating until I can say them right. Whenever she says Meshach, Miz Eula Thompson's rooster starts to crow and Sam Junior's laughing at this and he starts crowing with the rooster whenever Mamma says Meshach and a piece of biscuit's falling off his lip and Mamma's getting mad and calling him "Samuel Lee Jenkins Junior" like she does when he's cutting up, which is a lot of the time.*

They endure like hard-learned lessons—the memories of that day. They lodge in my mind like the railroad tie in the chinaberry tree. I had turned nine one week before. Mrs. Vera Spencer—a lady in Conrad that Mamma cleaned house for—had sewn me a new dress. Purple velvet with white lace around the collar and sleeves. I wore it that Sunday for the first time, hidden, to my great dismay, under the drab, hand-me-down coat that Mamma told me, for that third and final time, that I would wear until we got to church.

The church lay half-a-mile from our house along the red gravel road that traced the foot of the hill. Frame houses balanced on cinder block piers lined the road on both sides except for a few places where the road came too close to the base of the rise for a house to fit. Most were plain shotgun tin-roofed houses that had never seen a coat of paint. They all had some semblance of a porch, which was as necessary to life under the hill as nectar to hummingbirds. In the late afternoons of the spring and summer, and especially in the fall, those porches would throb with life, the men gathering on one to show off the drums and cats caught in the river and to tell lies over strong whisky about the ones that got away and about other less innocent pursuits. And the women, gathering on another to talk about the men and to watch the children run up and down the road and climb the red-clay bank to where they could look out past the edge of their existence and dream on things beyond catching lightning bugs in jars on sweltering summer nights and kicking footballs in the red dust of the dry fall air. But this day it was winter and the porches were empty of all but the wind, and the gray smoke from the chimneys lay on the cold air like heavy canvas, and the taste of the smoke was acrid and strong against the tongue.

*Now the sun is out and the wind has died down. The gray clouds are gone and the shadows of the trees are sharp against the ground and the ice puddles in the road are melting at the edges. A wren is singing from up ahead. Sam Junior says he's singing to me—that he's singing "you-stu-PID, you-stu-PID, you-stu-PID." Mamma tells him to hush—that a wren would never sing such a thing to any girl. Boss walks with us and chases after a stick that Sam Junior keeps throwing and Boss keeps bringing it back for Sam*

*Junior to throw again. When we get to where the road that runs up the hill to Jackdaw Street meets our dirt road, Willie is waiting for us, his gray whiskers prickling from his cheeks and chin. Willie lives near where the roads come together and we meet him here every Sunday. Sometimes he wears overalls but today he has on dark pants and a heavy coat with fur around the collar. Mamma smiles when we meet him. He's got chewing gum for Sam Junior and me. Sometimes Willie comes to the house at night and eats supper with us. He teases me and calls me Sugar Puff. He tries to tease Sam Junior too—says to him, "Boy, ain't you a pistol ball"—but Sam Junior won't play along. I unbutton my coat to show Willie my new dress. "My goodness, that sho do look pretty now, Sugar Puff," he says. "Boys gone be chasing after you like flies to honey when they sees you in that." When he smiles at me his strong white teeth shine in the sunlight. Some of them have gold rims that sparkle like mica. Mamma takes his hand and we walk on toward the church. Sam Junior runs ahead calling for Mose Jackson. Boss turns back toward the house—this is as far as he ever comes. Mamma and Willie are talking about Pastor Briarwood. Pastor Briarwood's the smartest man I know. And famous too. Got his picture on the front page of the Montgomery Advertiser this past November. Miz Sistrunk, my third grade teacher, brought a paper to school and showed us. He was standing right there with Miz Rosa Parks and another preacher named King. Miz Sistrunk told us how some court up in Washington said that now we could all ride the same buses as the white folks and didn't have to give up our seats to them. I've only been to Montgomery once and I've never ridden a bus but it made me real happy to hear this. I know that Pastor Briarwood had something to do with it and I'm glad I go to his church.*

* * *

Dr. Milligan settles into the soft leather desk chair, looks down at the file on his desk, avoiding eye contact. I know what this means. An instant later, he raises his eyes. They are heavy, severe eyes. His voice is even and holds no emotion. Just the facts. The cancer is advancing. We could try increasing the chemotherapy, feeding more of the toxin into William's tiny veins. If he still doesn't respond, there are other drugs. Options become more limited. But there is still hope. We mustn't lose hope.

* * *

We remember because we have no choice. My mind's path is random and uncertain and I am unable to steer it through the past and choose what images to share rainy afternoons with or what visions to carry to my bed while I wait for sleep. A child once so alive—suckling the milk from my breast, or bicycling down oak-shrouded streets in faded denim and boysweat and free laughter. Or lying on white sheets, bag hung high above, drip, drip, dripping through clear plastic tubes—dripping hopelessly into his wasted arm. And then fragrant soft stillness, closed eyes, the hands so tiny, prayerfully folded over the chest, the sweet floral smell everywhere, so many colors, so many sweet embraces, so much to remember. Too much to forget.

And then there is Willie Cline, strong and gentle, giving out chewing gum to children whenever he had it and warm smiles whenever he didn't, his oak-thick arms hanging loosely at his side, confessions of years of work as a pulpwooder. I think of those arms and believe he could have raised a car off the ground with them if he'd ever had need to. There was a comfort that spun from his full eyes and a power within them that a child could feel. I have always believed that he saw things with those eyes that other folks didn't see and that whatever he was looking at was more peaceful and rich than anything earthly. It was as if the physical world were transient for him, only a way-station on a journey to places truer. I have known many people who could deny, with absolute conviction, the ultimate reality of the corporal world. It is an effective means of easing life's burdens—of sanding the surface of tragedy to a smooth and palatable finish. I have always suspected that theirs was a denial born, unrealized, of the superficial comfort it gave rather than an abiding faith in something eternal. With Willie Cline, it was different. It seemed to me then, and it still does now, that whatever he held within those eyes would endure beyond any of us and even beyond all of the scattered fragments of hopes and dreams that we hatched and nurtured in that narrow strip of land between the bluff and the river.

I'm good at learning, but some things are not meant to be taught. A scholarship to Tuskegee Institute, a few dollars earned in a bookstore between classes, even a little help from Mrs. Vera Spencer, and it all adds up to a college education. But knowledge has failed me in the search for that repository where I might bury those rising agonies that dance untamed through the mind's eye and I have not learned what Willie Cline knew—have not discovered that bottomless abyss into which I may cast those images that for comfort's sake are better off forgotten.

*We walk on and the sky clouds up except it's not like usual and the clouds are different—not light fluffy puffs like clouds are supposed to be but mean, heavy low-hanging globs of darkness. And the smoke is not the chimney-smoke from the houses but it's different too and it tastes bitter in my mouth. We hear people up ahead. There is a group coming toward us and some are running. Sam Junior is running with Mose Jackson. They look scared, the two of them together, in a way I've never seen before. Now I can see the faces of the grownups and they are not the happy faces of Sunday morning but they look different and out of place. Their eyes are wide and strange. They walk too fast—not like Sunday-morning walking. Their loud voices are pitched high and shrill and I can't make out what they're saying. Mamma says, 'Oh Lord' and starts to cry and Willie puts his arm around her and we walk on.*

*At the place where the church used to be, the ground is black and smoke is coming off the ground. Black beams of smoking wood lean against each other where one wall used to be—right behind where Pastor Briarwood stands when he preaches. They look shaky—like they're about to fall. Some of the women are crying. Pastor Briarwood is standing with several of the men. He is looking at the ground and shaking his head slowly from side to side. One of the men has his arm on Pastor Briarwood's back. The men have strong anger in their eyes. Mamma is crying softly and Willie holds her closer while he puts his other big hand on my shoulder. Then I hear car tires crunching in the dirt. The brown colored car with a round light on top pulls up near to where Pastor Briarwood and some of the men are standing. A man in a heavy tan jacket gets out and walks over to Pastor Briarwood. His thick white hands stick out from the sleeves and he has a round face and short hair that's flat across the top. His cheek sticks out on one side like he's chewing a hickory nut. I can't see his eyes because of the dark glasses. When he talks to Pastor Briarwood, I can see his breath on the air. He has a notebook in his hand and is writing something down. He walks around where the church used to be, talking to Pastor Briarwood and writing and spitting out strands of dark brown juice. Pastor Briarwood is looking down while they walk—just looking at the ground and shaking his head. Now I feel the wetness in my eyes and I'm not sure why it's there. I look at Mamma, then at Willie. The water in my eyes makes everything look bent so I wipe them clean. Willie pulls me closer. He is looking straight ahead to where the church used to be. I can feel him looking far beyond where the church was—looking past all of the distance that my own eyes can reach and the whites of his eyes are full like a faraway sound is calling to him and it seems I can hear the echoes of it and I can feel how his jaw is set in place like steel and though his hand is on my shoulder, it seems like he's not even here with us—like he's a thousand miles away and yet it seems that he knows more about this one moment than all the rest of Creation and there is a calmness—not an anger at all but a peacefulness—that makes me feel better, makes me feel stronger with my shoulder under his big hand. When I look at his face, I remember Mamma telling about Daniel when King Darius had him thrown into the lion's den and I'm thinking about how Daniel must have looked when they led him to the lions and thinking that he probably looked a lot like Willie—like he knew something that nobody else knew—like he knew that everything was somehow going to be all right.*

There are days now when my life seems like a series of spaces connected by ever dwindling patches of failing reality. Spaces where love once resided, spaces where long-forgotten passions no longer burn, spaces where beloved memories have faded like cheap fabric in summer sunlight. I have come to know about spaces and of the emptiness they hold—and of how, on those increasingly rare occasions when memory can reach back into time and squeeze drops of hope from the past, a space can be filled.

There is a space between the beaten and the defeated.

It is a very small space in some people—almost infinitesimal. But it can also be vast—as boundless as the whole of the human spirit—and it affords, for those who know it, a comfort that most of us can barely imagine. Or perhaps, in the case of a nine-year-old girl, can share for a fleeting second.

Fifty-four years, two hundred and more changes of seasons, and I have collected more sadness within me than my soul can shed, and the half-forgotten sorrows hover soft above my heart like the shadow of a broken-winged sparrow. I will visit his grave tomorrow. I don't go as often now, but tomorrow I will. Standing at the footstone, I will look to the east and study the scant inscriptions in the tiny marble monolith, though I know the words by heart. I will breathe the past into my lungs, feel the late-afternoon sun against my back and watch my shadow fall over the small plot of ground, and stillness will rise out of the heartless earth like peace. I will reach for that space that Willie Cline knew and think of tomorrow, and of the next day, and of the next. And if the stillness holds, I might feel that distant comfort riding against me, weaving into the sun's warmth and pulling me ever so gently away from the edge of defeat's final precipice as I stand there alone, a tiny speck of humankind silhouetted against the falling sun.